SHE RECOGNIZED HIM INSTANTLY. His face was the same, if more mature, with tiny time lines etched into his brow and at the corners of his eyes. Flecks of silver whispered through his thick sable hair. Though thinner than he'd been when she'd seen him last, he was every bit as tall and broad of shoulder. And his intensity hadn't lessened.

"Jordanna Kirkland," he stated, dredging her name from the depths of the past as he soberly stared at the woman whose arrival at the campground had coincided nearly perfectly with his own.

Letting her frame pack slide the length of her leg until it stood on the ground, she struggled to contain her shock and its attendant rush of memories. "Lance."

"It's Patrick now. Patrick Clayes." Dragging his eyes from hers, he extended a hand to each of the other four members of the group in turn. "I'll be your guide."

"Larry Earls," said the first, a slim, pale man.

"Donald Scheuer," was the response of his taller, more heavyset companion.

"John Kalajian," the third said with a nod, an attractive professorial type.

"Bill Wennett," declared the last, the hint of arrogance in his voice echoing his cocksure stance.

All looked to be in their early forties and, from the similarity of their dress and gear, friends. It wasn't quite what Jordanna had expected when Craig Talese had so gallantly offered her his place on the trek.

Scrupulously avoiding Patrick's gaze, she looked from one man to the next. She had their undivided attention. "How many others will be joining us?" she asked quietly, assuming the women to be lagging somewhere behind. The names Scheuer and Wennett were ones Craig had mentioned; she was with the right group.

John looked at Larry; Donald's gaze met Bill's. Then all four looked with dawning dismay at Patrick, who finally spoke. "I was told there would be five of you. I guess this is it."

"There *were* supposed to be five of us. Who's she?" Bill demanded, turning an imperious eye on Jordanna.

She raised her chin a fraction of an inch. She'd learned to deal with high-handed men long ago. "Patrick had my name right. It's Jordanna Kirkland."

"Where's Craig?" Larry asked.

"He got an emergency call from San Diego. His daughter is ill. He flew out last night."

"So he called *you*?" Donald barked in disbelief.

"Yesterday," she stated.

"And you decided to join a group of men for five days in the wilds?" This from Bill again, with unmitigated disdain.

She stiffened her spine. "I had no idea I was joining a group of men. That must have been Craig's idea of a little joke." It fitted. Though as her accountant he was second to none, he was forever ribbing her about what he called her "male instinct" in the world of business.

"It's a lousy joke," Larry muttered. To Jordanna he seemed more threatened than angry at her presence.

Not so Donald. Anger punctuated his every word,

though his attention jumped from one to the other of his friends in search of support. "More than that. It's impossible! This was supposed to be a fun week with the guys. Totally uninhibited. There's no way we can have that with her along."

Jordanna's lips quirked at the corners. "Don't let me stop you. You can be as uninhibited as you want. I've seen a lot in my time. You won't shock me."

Donald ignored her. "What in the hell did Craig have in mind?"

For the first time since announcing his name, John spoke up. His voice was quiet, his manner philosophical. "Maybe he wanted to knock a hole in the last bastion of male chauvinism. You know how he's always after us." His pensive gaze slid to Jordanna. "Jordanna Kirkland...as in Willow Enterprises?"

Time reversed itself. It was as though she were once more standing before the skeptical bank board that would decide whether to grant her that crucial loan to bolster her fledgling business. As she'd done then, she now donned her most serene and confident expression. "That's right."

"You're its president?" John queried.

"And founder," she added, her pride present if understated.

Donald cursed, but he had the grace to do it softly. There his civility ended. "So she's the one he's been raving about all this time?" When John nodded, he scowled. "Then the joke's on us. Man, how could he do this?"

"Must be his warped sense of humor," Bill countered, looking as disgusted as his friend.

"I'll say."

"Kind of funny, when you think of it," John mused, only to draw three irate glances. He shrugged and held up a hand in self-defense. "Just kidding, guys. Just kidding."

"But what are we going to do about it?" Larry asked.

"She can't come, that's all there is to it," Donald barked.

Bill seconded the motion.

John had the good sense to keep his mouth shut.

By this time Jordanna was incensed. "What do you mean, she can't come?" she demanded. "She's here, in case you hadn't noticed. She's traveled six hours to get here, not to mention the time it took to make arrangements to be out of the office for the week. She's reimbursed Craig for the money he chipped in with you guys and she has her gear packed, and—" her eyes stopped flashing long enough to eye the foursome solemnly "—she's probably in far better shape for this hike than any of you."

Bill gave her the once-over, very slowly, then raised a brow and drawled, "Wouldn't surprise me in the least." His eyes narrowed. "But you have to wonder why a woman would want to go off into the woods with five men."

Jordanna didn't flinch. "You're being offensive," she stated quietly, then turned her head toward their guide for the first time since the fray had begun. And for the first time, she felt a true surge of anxiety. The four other men didn't daunt her in the least. For the past ten years, she'd fought their type. Though self-centered, they were predictable; though unpleasant, relatively harmless. Lance Clayes was something else. He was the link to a past she'd just as soon forget.

The way he was staring at her didn't help. She saw what he saw, fragments of those days of glory. And she saw something more. In the instant before he shuttered his gaze, she saw curiosity, perhaps a touch of respect, but also an undeniable flicker of heat. It unsettled her as the men's outward hostility had not done.

Slowly Patrick straightened, his dark brown eyes now harder as they held Jordanna's. "You're determined to come?"

"Yes."

"Do you know what you're getting in for?"

"I've read the trip description."

"And you think you can keep up?"

"I know I can."

"Have you ever backpacked before?"

Taking a calculated risk, she tipped her head toward the others. "Have they?"

The silence from the four was answer aplenty. If they'd been experienced backpackers, they would no more have hired a guide than have chosen to wear spanking new hiking boots. Not that hers were any more broken in, but they were softer, a gentle offshoot of the traditional heavy leather clods, more sneaker than boot. Indeed, part of her mission was to test their wearability; they wouldn't hit the market for another four months.

Patrick ran his tongue around the inside of his cheek, carefully choosing his words. "I was told you were all beginners," he said, shifting his gaze to the men.

Jordanna answered with a self-confidence none of the others could muster. "We are." She'd learned early on that being forthright about her weaknesses enhanced her strengths. "But we're determined." She ignored four scathing looks. "And ready to go." Innocently she scanned the faces of the men, then spoke with mock sweetness. "We were to be off by one, weren't we?"

"Yeah," Bill grumbled, turning to lift his pack.

"Hold on," Patrick cautioned as he loped off toward the Jeep parked near the other cars on the fringe of the campground. "I've got the supplies here," he called over his shoulder. "We'll have to divvy them up." With a minimum of effort he hauled first his own pack, then three open cartons filled with food and equipment from the back of the Jeep. "Bring your packs over. It'll be easier."

The five did as told, then watched him apportion supplies among six packs. It was with mild dismay that Jordanna watched the proceedings, praying that she'd have enough room in her pack for everything he gave her. She'd followed Craig's instructions to the letter, had even rushed out and bought as many books as she could find on backpacking, several of which had included step-by-step guides for filling a frame pack. Three times she'd loaded and unloaded the nylon-duck bag that sat so innocently atop its aluminum frame; each successive time the bag had looked less innocent. How something so roomy when empty could hold so little when filled was beyond her. But she'd persevered, discarding an additional item or two of clothing with each round of packing, until she'd finally found the right combination.

Mercifully, she'd had no trouble placing numerous bags of freeze-dried food in the top of her pack, or stuffing other goodies into side pockets. There were raisins, nuts, freeze-dried coffee and Tang, each carefully packaged in plastic bags for a minimum of bulk and weight. The latter was crucial. When every compartment was securely closed, and her sleeping bag and Ensolite pad rolled and fastened at the top of the frame, she had a substantial load to challenge her fitness

For a second too long she eyed the pack. "Problems, Jordanna?" Bill goaded. "Look too heavy?"

"I can handle it," she answered calmly.

Donald joined his friend and ally. "You're sure?" He shook his head, his mien patronizing, to say the least. "You can change your mind now before we get going. Once we're on the trail it won't be so easy. It'd be unfair to ask one of us to walk all the way back here with you."

Jordanna simply smiled. "We'll see who tires when," she said softly, then turned to her pack and contemplated the simplest way to put it on. The problem was taken out of her hands when Patrick easily lifted it and held it out. Turning, she slipped her arms through the straps, then, head down, fumbled with the hip belt. When she straightened, he was before her to adjust the shoulder straps.

Given the silence among the rest of the men, she wasn't sure whether to be grateful or annoyed. Patrick's assistance did nothing either for her own peace of mind or for the image of competence she was trying to project. In a way it was patronizing. Yet when she met his gaze there was neither smugness nor any semblance of a leer. Rather there was a dark intensity, a hardness reminiscent of the Lance Clayes of old. A muscle jumped in his jaw. Underdog or not, he was a man of determination.

"You can manage, can't you?" he asked quietly enough to spare her embarrassment, yet firmly enough to suggest his own doubt.

Jordanna was only marginally aware that the others had begun to don their packs. Her attention was riveted to Patrick. "Of course I can manage," she said, wondering why her voice didn't sound as firm as her conviction.

"The pack's heavy."

"I'm strong."

"We'll be going a long way, some of it over rough terrain."

"I've been running better than thirty miles a week for the past four years."

He showed no sign of being impressed, but simply continued to stare at her, into her, through her.

"I can do it, Lance—"

"Pat."

"Pat. Even if his sense of humor *is* a little off, Craig would never have suggested I come if he hadn't had faith in me." She took a breath, then stated baldly, "His job's at stake."

"What does he do?"

"He's my accountant."

For several seconds longer, Patrick studied her. His expression grew strangely wary. "You're a successful woman, Jordanna. Why are you here?"

"Can't successful women go on backpacking trips?" she countered, trying to make light of his query and the very powerful presence behind it.

"Sure they can," he asserted softly. "More often, though, they choose a week of leisure at one resort or another." His gaze clouded. "It's odd. Jordanna Kirkland. Peter's wife—"

"Peter's *ex*-wife," she corrected in a half whisper. "We've been divorced for nearly ten years. Our paths rarely cross. And who I was then has no bearing whatsoever on my presence here today."

He considered her quiet vehemence for an instant before silently turning away. Perplexed, Jordanna watched him hoist his own pack to his back. She sensed there would be far more to say about the past before the five days were done, and she wondered if she would be wise to turn back while she could. Patrick's presence shook her; she felt oddly unbalanced. If only she had an inkling as to the thoughts running through his mind...

Then she caught herself and brought her chin up. On principle alone she was determined to see the week through. She had decided to come; she had spent the past thirty-six hours making arrangements. And neither four reluctant men nor one Patrick Clayes was going to stop her.

Standing idly, waiting for the others to adjust their packs, she surveyed the surroundings only her peripheral vision had previously absorbed. In the parking area stood just four vehicles, two for the four buddies, Patrick's Jeep and her own rented Chevy. It seemed they'd have the woods to themselves—not surprising given the fact that it was early November. The foliage seekers had long since retreated to the warmth of their homes for the winter.

Though only partially bare, the trees wore their remaining leaves like shabby cloaks shedding threads here and there in the afternoon breeze. Beyond, the evergreens stood tall and grand in anticipation of their coming days of supremacy over those whose beauty was more ephemeral.

Two trails led into the woods from the parking area. Having studied the trip description long hours into the night, Jordanna knew they'd be taking the Basin Trail and making a large, rugged loop covering nearly twenty-two miles before returning on the Wild River Trail.

"Okay, listen a minute," Patrick began, gathering them all around for preliminary instructions. "First off, we travel as a group. The trails are well marked and hard to miss, but I don't want to risk losing any of you. We'll stay on the beaten path. No bush-whacking. Zero-impact hiking is what it's all about. When we disband Friday night, there should be no sign whatsoever that we've ever been here. Side trips through the brush will only destroy the natural beauty of the place. None of us want to do that," he stated positively as he looked from one to another of his charges. To Jordanna's relief, his gaze touched her but briefly.

"Our walking time this afternoon will be roughly two hours, though with stops here and there we probably won't reach the Blue Brook shelter until dinnertime. It's a perfect walk for beginners. But—" he paused, a warning look on his face "—if anyone has trouble, *any* trouble, I want you to yell. If your pack is killing you, it might need a simple adjustment. Same with your boots. At the first sign of blisters, we stop to apply moleskin. At the first problem with a knee or an ankle, we put on an Ace bandage. Since none of you have backpacked before, there are bound to be aches and pains, but—within limits—I want you to speak up. This is a pleasure trip. We don't need martyrs. We're not looking for heroes. A problem dealt with early on can be easily handled. Down the road it may be a little harder. Understood?" He cast a glance from one intent face to another. When each had nodded, he eased up. "Any questions?"

Jordanna had a million questions. Where do we sleep? How do we cook? What if it rains? Will there be bears? But, like the others, she shook her head, confident that the answers would be forthcoming in time.

"Let's go," he said. "I'll lead the way. John, you take up the rear. We'll switch around once you all get the hang of it."

Without further ado, he set off. Jordanna watched his retreating form, admiring the way his gear seemed an extension of his body, wondering how long he'd been backpacking. Judging from the spring in his step, he loved it.

"Jordanna?"

John's quiet call drew her from her momentary preoccupation. With a start she realized the others were already on the trail. Flashing him a buoyant smile that she hoped would cover for her lag, she moved quickly ahead.

Though the air was brisk, it wasn't cold. Having

checked the long-range forecast, Jordanna knew that there were no major storms expected. Chills she could easily withstand; the clothes she wore were designed to be lightweight and warm. Snow, though, she could do without. She was no glutton for punishment.

The path was of crushed stone leading southward past several deserted campsites before entering deeper woods. She concentrated on walking steadily and shifted her pack once to a more comfortable position. She was grateful she hadn't skimped in selecting her gear; her shoulder straps were well padded, her hip belt substantial enough to evenly distribute the load. Amazing what she'd learned about backpacking in such little time, she mused. She only hoped her cramming would pay off further along. Going to bed at 2:00 A.M. hadn't been the smartest thing to do, particularly since she'd awoken at six to shower and dress and head out from New York. She would be tired tonight. But then, evenings on the trail were probably going to be quiet and early ones.

Few words were spoken as the six walked on, each seeming too awed by the silent splendor of the woods to shatter its effect. They had left all civilization behind. Even the path was now of packed earth strewn with leaves. Larry, the photographer of the group, paused to take pictures from time to time. When he stopped to adjust his pack, Patrick assisted him while the others rested, occasionally sipping from canteens or flexing cramped shoulders.

On the move once more, they came to a wetter area of ground, where a plank walkway had been constructed.

"Someone was thoughtful," Larry observed.

"We'll run across these from time to time," Patrick explained, tapping his booted toe against the

first of the planks. "But they're not first and fore-
most for our benefit."

"Then whose?" Bill asked irreverently.

"The earth's," Patrick answered. "Walkways like
these retard soil erosion. Without them, some of the
trails would be impassable, not to mention devoid of
vegetation." Without awaiting further comment, he
went ahead. The others followed. What had been the
symphonic rustling of dead leaves underfoot became
a more percussive series of thuds as they progressed.

Head down now, Jordanna studied the planks,
then the soggy ground to either side as her professional instinct went to work. She wondered how her
hiking shoes would hold up on wet ground. Had
Patrick's words not rung fresh in her ear, she might
have been tempted to step off into the muck. But his
words had hit their mark, and besides, she was
hemmed in front and rear by men who would delight in any slip she made. A soggy shoe was not the
most auspicious adjunct to a hike. Perhaps at the
end of the trip, she decided, when no great harm
could be done, she'd experiment.

On dry ground once again, they climbed steadily
along what Patrick announced to be Blue Brook until they reached a footbridge. There, at his direction,
they lowered their packs for a rest. At first Jordanna
was startled. They'd been walking for barely an
hour. Only when she set her pack on the ground
and straightened did she understand his motive.
Though she thought herself in the best of shape,
there seemed to be tiny muscles in her back that
she'd never felt before. Stretching carefully, she
eased down onto a nearby rock to savor the sight of
the gurgling brook below.

The men talked among themselves. She sat apart,
perfectly comfortable with the distance. Solitude
was a treat for her, given the number of people who

rushed in and out of her working life. If the others left her to her own musings during the trek, she wouldn't mind in the least.

"Everything okay?"

She looked up to find Patrick shading her from the sun.

"Fine," she answered quickly, her gaze darting back to a gentle cascade splashing into a pool. "It's really beautiful."

His eyes followed hers. "It's just the beginning. This season is the best. Minimum people, maximum nature."

Something in his tone said that he appreciated solitude as she did. Looking up, she studied the rugged planes of his face. He was unfairly handsome; time had served him well. "Do you—" she swallowed involuntarily and began again "—do you do this often?"

He continued to stand beside her, legs braced wide. His dark hiking pants were well worn and fitted him comfortably. She sensed pure muscle beneath. "Backpacking? Whenever I can."

"Guiding," she corrected, tutoring her thoughts away from his thighs. She wondered if he earned his living as an outdoorsman. Scanning her memory, she couldn't recall having heard about him in recent years. But then, she realized, the mind did strange things. For years she'd blotted out anything and everything to do with football. She might have seen something in the paper and never taken it in.

Eyes trained upstream, he didn't spare her a glance. "Nah. I only take groups out once or twice a year, usually in late fall or early spring. When I go myself, it's into more remote areas, ones I've never seen before."

"You're an explorer then?"

"Mmm." As though loath to say more, he abruptly turned and wandered to a nearby boulder. Lithely hiking himself upon it he wrapped his arms around his knees to enjoy the scene a while longer.

Staring after him, Jordanna wondered just what path he had taken in life. His playing days were over; forty-year-old quarterbacks were not exactly in demand. If he'd turned to coaching, he'd hardly have been able to take off for a week at the height of the season. On the other hand, he might well have entered broadcasting, where his presence on the weekend would suffice. He was eloquent; his initial speech to the group had proved that. And if the private type, he was hardly shy. Yet in the old days he had avoided the press. Peter had been the one to court them with every bit of charm he could manage, and that was considerable, she remembered with a scowl.

But she didn't want to think of Peter. Or Lance. *Or* the old days.

With a deep breath she lowered her gaze. Her fingers idly slid through the dried brush by her side, but the startling image in her mind's eye was of a softer, more vibrant brush, that of the dark hair peeping through the open neck of Patrick's shirt as she'd seen it moments before. Stunned, she frowned, then reached for a dead leaf and crushed it along with the unbidden image. Refocusing on the enchantment of the stream, she let her mind trip pleasantly until, at length, Patrick hopped down from his perch and retrieved his pack in silent example to the others. With the wave of his hand, they were off again.

Bathed in the relief of having donned her pack alone, Jordanna felt fresh of mind and decidedly confident. Eyes alert, she took in everything, from the pines swaying rhythmically above to the solid firs more stoically enduring the intrusion of humanity.

The cliffs that banked the far side of the stream were granite slabs slicing neatly into the water, where, over ages, they were gentled by the crystal-clear flow.

When the path took a turn upward, her legs were tested for the first time. She welcomed the exertion, enjoying the stretch as she always did in her early morning warm-ups. She found something intrinsically refreshing in the reminder that her body was far more than a machine to be taken for granted. Being well oiled took work. She liked testing her limits and even now lengthened her stride until she clearly felt the muscles of her thighs and calves. This appreciation of the physical was but one of the ways Willow Enterprises had benefited from its founder.

As if in reminder, she touched her cheek, then reached back into a lower side pocket of her pack for a small tube of cream. Makeup was her specialty; indeed, cosmetics for the sports-minded woman had been the first order of business after Willow Enterprises' founding. Its product line was extensive, and though it included the colorful creams and shadows desired by the fashion-conscious woman, its pride was a more practical line of moisturizing agents. The dab of cream now in her palm was one of these. She smoothed it across the backs of her hands and around her fingers, then applied the excess to her cheeks and chin in a motion that might have been a simple soothing of flesh had any of the men noticed. Five days in the wilds without benefit of other makeup would put the cream to the test, as would the sun, even weak as it was, its protective qualities.

Without missing a step, she comfortably kept her place in the casual line, breathing deeply of the scent of fall. Clusters of birches, their yellow leaves now pale and withering, had sprung up to share the forest with beeches and firs. High above, the cry of migrating geese echoed amid the breeze.

"You look more spring than fall," John commented, startling her as he drew abreast of her.

She glanced down at her outfit, a stylish, lightly padded jacket cuffed at the waist and wrists, with matching pants that tapered, then zippered at the ankles. She was lime green from collar to heel.

With a soft chuckle, she concurred. "It was a choice of this, bright yellow, soft pink or lavender. Somehow I thought the green would blend better with the woods."

"Isn't that a jogging suit?"

"Pretty much so, though we're marketing it as an all-purpose sports outfit. The principles are the same. Loose and light but insulating. Actually, this jacket is warmer than a regular running shell. I'm really comfortable." She looked far more so than any of the men, she admitted to herself with a certain amount of smugness. Their hiking jackets and pants were a sight heavier. Only Patrick with his anorak looked fully at ease.

"Not bad," John decided, then fell back several steps once more.

Jordanna did feel comfortable, surprisingly so. She'd packed a heavy wool sweater, but she was counting on multiple layers of lighter coverings to keep her warm. Walking was one thing; despite the growing chill in the air as the afternoon wore on and the sun paled and dipped, she actually felt tiny trickles of perspiration on her back beneath her pack. When the day's walk was done and they sat idle, ah, that would be a different matter.

"How's it going back there?" Patrick called from the front of the line. Three other heads swiveled around with his.

"Just fine," Jordanna assured them all with a smile.

"Blisters?" Donald suggested.

"Nope."

"Sore shoulders?" Bill hinted.

She shook her head. "Sorry. Of course, if you guys are tired—"

Just as abruptly as they'd looked back, all three faced forward again and moved on. Only Patrick lingered for a moment's study of her serene expression. Then he too whipped around and was off.

The remainder of the afternoon's trek was pleasant and promising. Tuning out the men's chatter, Jordanna derived from the outdoors the gratification she sought. The gentle sounds of the wild, the random rustle of tiny woodland creatures, the sweet scent of spruce—all were a soothing balm against the memory of the city's bustle.

Her body held up well; she smiled to herself when, behind her, John began to grunt as the trail climbed toward a ridge. When at last they reached the shelter where they'd be spending the night, she silently congratulated herself on a job well done.

Half an hour later she began to wonder if her congratulations had been premature. It had been one thing when they were walking, single file for the most part, and she could easily lose herself to the joy of the forest. Stationary now, idly studying the three-sided log shelter, she let herself think for the first time of the awkwardness such closeness could present for a woman among five men.

They'd all lowered their packs and were relaxing while Patrick set up the camp stove to heat water for hot drinks before dinner. A stream just north of the shelter was their water supply; he'd shown them the way before he'd set to work. Now there was little to do but relax until the business of making dinner began.

As had happened during the afternoon, the men talked among themselves, ignoring Jordanna as much as possible. She studied them as she sat on the ground, then reached into her pack to change into a pair of soft moccasins. She wore two pairs of socks, a thin inner pair and an outer pair of thicker wool rag. Her feet were toasty, though she still felt chilled. Digging into the pack again, she pulled out a heavy wool cap and tugged it on over her stylishly cropped thick chestnut hair.

She had settled back once more when Patrick suddenly moved from the stove to his own pack. As she watched, he shed his jacket and unbuttoned his shirt. She held her breath when the shirt came off to reveal corded shoulders and a lean torso. When he bent to fish into the pack, she was held by the play of his muscles, sinewed and firm, flexing grandly as he reached forward. Then he straightened and, as though physically touched by her gaze, slowly turned his head to look at her.

Jordanna felt a strange thudding in her chest. She tried to look away, but his dark eyes were locked to hers. Then, as slowly as he'd turned his head, he began to approach, stopping only when he was within arm's reach of her. His long-sleeved, insulated shirt hung limply from his fingers. With catlike grace, he lowered himself to his haunches.

"Anything wrong?" he asked softly.

She quickly shook her head and dropped her eyes, not altogether prudently, to the soft pelt of fur on his chest. He had to be cold, yet he looked warm and alive, making her, to her dismay, feel the same.

"You're sure?"

She swallowed hard and nodded. But her eyes clung to his flesh. Her fingers curled into her palms.

"You'll catch a chill," she whispered.

"Are you worried?" he returned in that same soft voice. It held a touch of silk this time, its smoothness shimmering into her.

"You're our leader," she managed. "It wouldn't help us if you got sick."

"I've got an iron constitution."

"So I see," she said, then willed the words erased. The flush that rose to her cheeks had little to do with the brisk early-evening air.

Then she caught sight of a pale scar at his shoulder and, without thinking, reached up to touch it. Patrick's flinch was involuntary but quickly controlled, and he held steady while her fingertip traced the mark.

"Battle scar?"

He hesitated a minute. When he spoke, his silken tone held grains of sand. "Of sorts. Throwing a football for years can do great things to a man."

"When...?"

He cleared his throat. "My last year. It made the decision to retire that much easier." His voice was devoid of bitterness, indeed of all emotion, in keeping with his eyes.

She nodded dumbly, unaware that her finger remained on his skin until he grabbed her hand and pressed it to his flesh, inching it downward and around the muscled swell of his chest. His flesh was firm beneath her palm, his heartbeat much more steady than her own. When her fingertip grazed his tight nipple, her gaze shot to his.

"Have a thing for jocks?" he asked on a velvet note of mockery. When she grabbed her hand away, he readily released it.

"That was unnecessary," she scolded unevenly.

He gave a one-shouldered shrug, then looked down and slid his arms onto the shirt. "It'd make sense. Peter...me...."

"You're almost as crude as Bill."

His eyes met hers as he raised the shirt, lifted his arms and eased his head through its collar. Jordanna

suspected the leisurely way he stretched into the
knit was deliberate; extended, his body looked all
the more powerful. His summer's tan lingered at-
tractively, only slightly paler beneath his arms amid
the soft, dark hair that sprouted there.

"Bill doesn't know you," he said, his voice muffled through the shirt.

"Neither do you!" she exclaimed, indignation rising to displace all thoughts.

Without hurry, he smoothed the shirt down over
his chest. "I know who you are."

"So do I. I'm Jordanna Kirkland of Willow Enterprises. Period."

His voice lowered and grew harder. "You're also
Peter Kirkland's ex-wife."

Jordanna studied him closely, her eyes growing
sharp. "That bothers you, doesn't it?"

"Why should it bother me?" he asked with a nonchalance that didn't extend to the telltale flex of his
jaw.

"Because you and Peter were rivals from the start.
Because Peter bested you once too often." Goaded by
instinct, she barreled on. "Because maybe, just maybe, you find me attractive."

His back suddenly ramrod straight, Patrick stared
at her for a minute. Then, with neither admission nor
denial, he rose and returned to his pack. As abruptly, Jordanna shifted to lie against her own, facing
away from the rest. Throwing an arm across her
eyes, she took a deep, calming breath and willed the
image of a lean, sun-bronzed chest to self-destruct.
When it refused to do so, she forced her mind back
to New York, burying her thoughts in Willow Enterprises as she'd done now for ten long years.

She wasn't sure if she dozed off, but when John
came to offer her a cup of coffee, she opened her eyes
with a start and sat up.

"Thanks," she said, mustering a weak smile.

"Tired?"

"A little. It's been a long day."

He hunkered down beside her to nurse his own hot brew. "You drove all the way from New York this morning?"

"Uh-huh."

"Then you must be dead. We all came up yesterday and slept late this morning."

She threw a cursory glance toward the others. "Have you families?"

"Three wives and seven kids among us. Bill's a bachelor."

"How do you know each other?"

"We were college friends."

This time her smile was more natural. "You're kidding! And you've stayed close all this time?"

"Actually, no. We went separate ways after graduation—Don to dental school, Bill to business school, Larry to work with his dad, Craig to get his CPA."

She took a sip of her coffee, savoring its warmth as it slid down her throat. "And you?"

"I went on for a Ph.D. in math. I teach now."

"Math," she mused. "Interesting." Then she frowned. "But how did you all get back together?"

"At our tenth reunion. We discovered we still had a lot in common, including an itch to get away for a week now and then." He laughed softly. "The first time we tried it, we went as couples to the Caribbean. None of the wives got along, and Bill's girl was an absolute pariah."

Jordanna's brows met in a sympathetic frown. "That's a shame."

"No, it was great." When her frown deepened in confusion, he explained. "What we *really* wanted, the guys, I mean, was a week away from *everything*—wives, girlfriends and kids as well as work.

So we started planning trips like these." He rocked back on his heels and rolled his eyes toward the darkening sky. "We've sailed in the Bahamas, skied in the Rockies, eaten our way through a cruise, lost our share in Las Vegas."

"But never backpacked before."

"Nope. Never that."

"How did you get hold of Patrick?"

"We didn't. Larry's travel agent did. She knew that he took groups out from time to time and gave him a call. That was last spring."

"You booked him that early? You must all be football freaks." Though she couldn't quite hide the scorn in her voice, John attributed it to a typical female disdain for the sport. His response was indulgent.

"As a matter of fact, one of our trips did combine four days in L.A. with the Super Bowl."

Her moan was not at all feigned. "Oh, God, then I'll have to listen to shoptalk all week?"

"No. That was a stipulation of Patrick's before he'd be our guide."

"What do you mean?"

"He won't discuss football. Apparently it's a standard rule of his." John grew more thoughtful. "I guess he'd had it by the time he retired." He shook his head wistfully. "Man, he was some player."

She scowled. "They didn't call him Lance for nothing."

"Mmm. He really shot that football down the field." As though suddenly realizing that Jordanna knew more than she let on, John eyed her curiously. "You knew him. You know football." When he paused, Jordanna held her breath. "Kirkland. You can't be related to...?"

There seemed no point in prevarication. Patrick had said it twice now; it was simply a matter of time until the others overheard. "Peter. I was married to him for three years. We've been divorced for ten."

"No kidding?" A broad smile split his face. "Hey, that's great! Not the divorce part, I mean. But the marriage. You must have been with him during the best of his playing years! That's exciting!"

"Not really," she stated. "As a matter of fact, it was pretty boring."

"You couldn't have thought so if you married him."

She sighed and looked down. "You're right. I didn't at first. But I learned pretty quick how...ach, it's not important." She raised her eyes to focus on Patrick, who seemed busy around the stove. "We should give him a hand," she mumbled, pushing herself to her feet. She had the fleeting image of jumping from the frying pan into the fire, but only knew that she had to let John know there were some things *she* wouldn't discuss.

Patrick looked up at her approach, his expression blank. It was a help.

"What can I do?" she asked, rubbing her cold hands together.

"You can dig the beef stew out of your pack. This water's nearly boiling."

By the time she returned with the packets, the other men had gathered round to watch the proceedings.

"You mean those little things are gonna fill us?" Donald asked, eyeing Jordanna's booty with dismay.

The small nearby lantern illumined Patrick's smirk. "You'll be filled. Believe me. I've allowed two portions for every man."

"Then we can divide up Jordanna's extra?" Bill asked, grinning at what he thought to be irresistible cleverness.

"Not on your life," Jordanna responded. "I'm eating."

"You'll get fat," Larry cautioned.

"Working as hard as you guys? No way."

Bill turned to Donald. "I think she should do the cooking. Woman's work and all."

"No wonder you're not married, Bill," Jordanna scoffed. "No woman in this day and age will have you."

Larry gave half a guffaw, then gulped when Bill scowled at him.

Patrick held up a hand. "Children. Please. Let's try to restrain ourselves. Everyone chips in when it comes to cooking. John and Donald, go on up to the stream and fill the extra pots with water. We'll put them on to heat while we're eating so we'll have something to clean up with later. Bill, I think the pudding's in your pack. I'll need it in a minute. Larry, you've got the plates and utensils. Jordanna, come over here and make the stew." He frowned. "And don't look at me like I'm the devil incarnate. You cook tonight and you're done for the week. Fair?"

The rebellion that was on the tip of her tongue instants before simply vanished. "Just tonight... then I'm done for the week?" she asked with a bargaining half smile.

"Uh-oh," Donald groaned, "she's a bra burner. The executive woman. She hates to cook."

Donning her most beatific smile, Jordanna knelt beside Patrick. "You instruct. I'll cook."

That was precisely what she did. Dinner was surprisingly good and decidedly filling. Patrick was patient, if all business, which pleased her no end. She'd begun to imagine that being near him for the week might be an ordeal above and beyond those memories she fought, but, during dinner at least, he treated her like one of the guys.

Later that night, well, that was something else.

2

EXHAUSTED, JORDANNA fell into a deep sleep shortly after dinner. Burrowing snugly into her sleeping bag in a far corner of the shelter, she was comfortably warm and dead to the world. The men talked and laughed, but she heard nothing until the middle of the night when, disturbed by an unexpected sound, she awoke with a start.

It took her a minute to remember where she was. Groggy, she looked around, then sat up and studied the darkness. When the noise came again, her head jerked toward the vague forms on the opposite side of the shelter.

Someone was snoring. She put a hand to her chest to still the thudding of her heart, then scowled and looked away. Peter had snored. More nights than she cared to recall she'd awoken to urge him onto his side. Then she'd lain awake for hours brooding, unable to fall back to sleep.

So now she was suddenly wide awake. The snoring persisted, a deep, crescendoing shudder that grated as she sat. She tried to make out who it was, but couldn't tell one sleeping bag from another in the dark—not that she would have been able to do anything had she known who the culprit was.

Annoyed at having been awakened, she drew her down-covered knees to her chin and glared out at the woods beyond the shelter, then back into the shadows. As her eyes slowly adjusted she deciphered one sleeping bag set apart from the others, lying roughly halfway between hers and theirs. It had to be Patrick's.

At least he wasn't the snorer, she mused, studying his dark cocooned form. Strange how he'd set himself there; perhaps not so strange in light of his job. He was the quarterback, calling the plays, ready to deal with any problem that might arise in the middle of the night. She gave a derisive snort. Perhaps he was afraid that one of the men might approach her. How touching. Her white knight, sound asleep.

With lips pressed tightly together she struggled to her feet and, sleeping bag and all, shuffled from the shadowed shelter out into the pale moonlight. Only when she'd gone far enough to reduce the snoring to a dull hum did she stop. Sinking down inside the sleeping bag, she sat cross-legged on the ground, her back to the shelter, her eyes on the nightscape.

Cast now in silver rather than gold, the woods were as beautiful as they'd been by day. She tipped her head back to study the branches overhead, then slowly returned her gaze to the ground. At a movement in the brush, she froze, watching wide-eyed when what appeared to be an opossum sauntered across her range of vision, leading with its pointed nose, trailing with its tail, disappearing into the woods with an indifference to her presence that she accepted with pure relief. Though adventurous, a physically active woman, she knew little about creatures of the wild. For an instant she wondered what else might wander about in the night—deer, fox, *bears*—then she quickly thought of Patrick and found solace knowing he was near. He seemed levelheaded and skilled when it came to the outdoor life; she admired him for that. Thoughts diverging, she also admired him for the ease with which he'd handled the group on this first day of the hike, for his deep, rich voice, for the firm tone of his body....

Her mind drifted and she was back in the colosseum stands, eyes glued to the teams in formation at the five-yard line. The crowd roared on either side, but beyond its thunder, her sole concentration was on the quarterback whose hands were ready, awaiting the snap. He turned his head to one side then the other, shouting coded commands to his team. Then he had the ball and ran back to pass, his padded shoulders bunched and broad, his hips sleek and lean. Jordanna had always responded to seeing him that way. Poised on the brink of action, he was, in her mind, the quintessential male.

Moments later, when, having failed to find a receiver, he'd barreled over the line to make the touchdown himself, he was lost to her. Arms raised in triumph, he'd belonged to the crowd, his adoring public and his own monumental ego.

Shaking her head in an attempt to chase these unbidden images from her mind, she hugged herself more tightly. Peter had been physically magnificent, both on the field and off. Emotionally, intellectually—those were other matters.

And what about Patrick? He was good-looking, she admitted reluctantly, too good-looking. And he affected her, which bothered her. She'd been unaffected by a man for years and had wanted it that way. Given the debacle of her marriage and the subsequent demands of the career she'd molded for herself, she had no time for men.

Her physical response to Patrick surprised her. Even now she could recall the feel of his skin beneath her hand, and her palm tingled. Was she sex starved? Or simply a masochist? *Did* she have a thing for jocks?

Moaning softly, she buried her face against her knees. Then she heard a footstep behind her and whirled to confront a dark form looming above.

When she would have cried out in fright, a large hand clamped over her mouth. A long arm curved around her middle. Strong thighs lowered to frame her hips.

"Shh. It's just me." The whisper faded. Slowly the hand from her mouth was withdrawn, fingers trailing across her lips in reluctant departure.

"Patrick?" she whispered, twisting to look up into his moon-shadowed face, in doing so dragging her head to his shoulder. His arm remained around her sleeping bag in the vicinity of her waist.

"Yes," he whispered. "Are you all right?"

Her pulse was racing. "You frightened me!"

"I heard you get up. I thought you had to go to the...well, when you didn't come back I got worried."

"I'm fine," she whispered, but wondered if it were true. Her nerve ends continued to jump. She made no move to free herself from his embrace, though. It was surprisingly comfortable, not binding, yet warm and supportive.

"Couldn't sleep?"

When she would have cast a glance toward the shelter, she found she couldn't take her eyes from his. "One of the men was snoring." The dim sound persisted. "It woke me up."

"Don't like snoring?" Given the lightness of his tone, she could have sworn he was teasing her.

"No."

"Peter didn't snore?"

Not teasing. Goading. Straightening, she freed herself from his arm and inched forward on her bottom until she sat a solid foot away. She stared off into the woods. "Peter snored."

"And you didn't like it."

"No."

For several moments there was silence. Then Patrick flipped to the side to sit on the ground by Jordanna's hip, facing in the opposite direction. She didn't look at him.

"Why are you here, Jordanna?" he asked at last, his voice still low but now hard and direct.

She knew he wasn't talking about the woods in the middle of the night. "You've asked that before. It's getting boring."

"I'd still like to know."

She did look at him then, but his profile was shadowed. "Why?"

"Curiosity."

"Curiosity killed the cat." She spoke to herself as much as to him. There were far too many questions on her mind.

His jaw flexed. She saw that much. "I'm not planning on dying just yet," he stated softly but firmly. "I've fought too hard for too long. Which brings me back to my question. Why have you come?"

She refused to be put on the defensive. "Why do *you* think I've come?"

"It's occurred to me," he began without hesitation, "that you knew I'd be leading this group."

"Are you kidding?"

"Shh!" He tossed a glance toward the shelter. "You'll wake the others."

Though she lowered her voice to a whisper, her incredulity remained. "You think I came because of *you*?"

"It's been done."

She threw her head back vehemently. "Omigod, I don't believe it! Another one! Pure ego!" Then she raised her head and stiffened her spine. "If I'd known you were going to be here, I'd *never* have come!" Her eyes flashed angrily, uncompromisingly.

"You hate me."

"What?"

He spoke more slowly, his eyes just as uncompromising in their hold on hers. "You hate me."

"I barely *know* you. How could I hate you?"

"You were the one who pointed out that Peter and I were rivals."

"What's that got to do with hate?"

"You were his wife. It'd be natural for you to side with him."

"Peter never hated you."

"No," he mused grimly. "I suppose you're right. Since he always came out on top, he'd have no reason to hate."

"But you do?"

"Hate? No. Resent...perhaps. It wasn't pleasant playing second fiddle to Peter Kirkland all those years.... But we're getting off the point."

"Which is?"

"Why, in your words, you'd never have come on this trip if you'd known I'd be along."

With a deep breath, she squeezed her eyes shut and lowered her head to her knees once again. "To be blunt, Patrick," she began, speaking slowly, as though with great effort, "I don't need the memories."

"Ahh. You've sworn off jocks."

Her head shot up. He was goading her again. "I was never *on* jocks," she stated ardently. "I was in love with Peter Kirkland, the man, *not* the jock."

"Could you separate the two?" he asked pointedly.

Her whisper was less steady. "I thought I could. At first."

"But not in the end?"

"We're divorced. It's over." She turned her head away. "And none of your business."

Undaunted, he gave a magnanimous sigh. "Well, that's a relief, at least."

"What is?" she murmured against the rim of her sleeping bag.

"That you're not into jocks. But you are into men?"

She whirled around. "I can't believe you said that."

"Why not? It's a simple question."

"It's crude."

"Like Bill. Ah, that's right. I remind you of Bill."

He didn't. Not in the least. And whether he was teasing or goading this time, she didn't know. "Why are you doing this?" she whispered. "Why don't you . . . go pick on someone your own size?"

"I like your size better." When she tried to rise, he shackled her arm through the bag and stayed her escape.

"Go talk to one of the men," she muttered.

"They're sleeping."

"Why aren't you?"

"Because you're not. Because I heard you get up. Because I was worried. And curious."

He inched closer. She could see that his hair was mussed, that his jaw was tight, that his gaze had dropped to her lips. When again she tried to pull back, he swung around to much the same position he'd been in when he'd captured her.

"Let me go, Lance," she whispered, struggling to steady the suddenly erratic beat of her heart. He was behind her, his warmth blanketing her back, his arms circling her front, holding her more gently than she wished. For, had he been rough, she might have fought. But this gentleness, this warmth was strangely seductive. Or was it the night? Or the allure of the woods? Or the fact that it had been a long, long time since she'd been held by a man?

"It's Patrick, Jordanna," he murmured against her hair. "Lance no longer exists; you needn't fight

memories with me. It's Patrick. And he's a man.
And, damn it—" his voice lowered "—he does find
you attractive."

When she should have been turned off by his begrudging admission, she was only further intrigued.
Suddenly she wasn't thinking of Lance or the past,
but of Patrick and the way his firm man's body
seemed to shield her from all else. She was thinking
of his chest, with its soft, dark hair, of his fingers,
smelling faintly musky as they'd brushed her lips, of
his eyes, deep brown and warm when he willed
them so.

Cupping her chin, he tipped her head to the side,
resting it in the crook of his shoulder in an open spill
of moonlight. His face mere inches away, he looked
at her then, studying each of her features in turn as
she lay, mesmerized, in his arms.

"I was curious," he began in a soul-stroking murmur, "about what it would be like to kiss you."

Only in that instant did Jordanna allow herself to
admit that she was curious about the very same
thing. Patrick Clayes was strong, eminently masculine, thoroughly appealing. When his head lowered
by inches until his lips were a hair's breadth from
hers, she held her breath, waiting, waiting to see if
the frisson of excitement shimmering through her
veins was an illusion.

It wasn't. His mouth whispered a kiss first on one
corner of her lips, then the other, and her heart beat
faster. Having expected a more forceful approach,
she was both startled and charmed by his gentle
evasion. The excitement she'd felt was joined by a
strange languor. Her limbs went weak. She closed
her eyes to better savor every soft nuance of his
touch.

His lips moved slowly, stringing the gentlest of
kisses along the line of her mouth until she thought

she'd scream in frustration. He was goading her. Or was he giving her time to demur? But she wasn't the demurring type. She knew what she wanted. It wasn't the sanest thing, but she did know.

Her lips parted, met seconds later by the fullness of Patrick's kiss. Like his voice it was rich and velvet smooth, like his skin, warm and alive. He moved his mouth with the same riveting gentleness with which his arms held her, drawing a response from her most feminine depths.

When he suddenly drew back, she was bereft, but only until she caught the smoldering gleam in his eyes. "Jordanna?" he whispered unsteadily.

In answer, she reached up, threaded her fingers through the thickness of his sleep-mussed hair and drew his head down until their lips met once more. This time she found the force she'd expected before, but far from brute, it was electrifyingly wonderful, satisfying the very need she felt. Raising a hand to her throat, he caressed its smooth line as his tongue sampled the more varied textures of her teeth, her gums, her seeking tongue. He was as breathless as she when they separated.

"You're so soft," he whispered against her temple as his hand continued to stroke her neck. He slid a finger beneath the crew neck of her thermal shirt and traced a gentle arc along her collarbone. "How come you're so soft?"

"My cream," she said unsteadily, her sole concentration on that finger that seemed, with each slow sweep, to inch lower. Her breasts were taut, upthrust, aching to be held.

"Your cream?" He looked down at her.

She swallowed hard under his lambent gaze. "Moisturizer. I'm an addict."

His hand came to a rest over the hollow of her throat. "For business?"

"For me. I like taking care of myself."

He dropped his hand, but left his arm around her back. "Is that a hint?"

"I hadn't meant it to be," she said, sobering now that the lure of his touch seemed a dream, "but I suppose it's true."

"You're independent."

"Yes."

"No leaning on a man?"

"Not anymore." Left unspoken was direct comment on her marriage. Patrick seemed willing to let the matter ride.

"Surely you've been involved with men since Peter."

"Why surely?"

He studied her for several moments. Then he let out a sigh of resignation and, as if he'd forgotten her question, spoke on a different tack. "You're a beautiful woman, Jordanna. I always envied Peter. You made him look good."

She sat up slowly. "Funny, I thought it was the other way around."

"No way. He may have had the trophies, but you had the class. Your business is proof of that."

"You know about my work?"

He donned an endearingly sheepish expression. "Only what I overheard the guys saying tonight."

She scrunched up her face. "You mean that while I slept they were *talking* about me?"

The gentle finger he placed on her lips quieted her more so even than his soft, "Shh. They needed to let off steam. A couple of them are still pretty miffed that you insisted on coming along."

"Tough," she spat, but in a whisper. "They're a bunch of—"

"Uh-uh. Be generous. They feel awkward. That's all."

"Do you?"

"What do you think?"

"I don't know. I don't know you at all."

"Are you sorry...that happened?"

She knew he was referring to their kiss, and could be nothing but truthful. It was her way. "No," she answered softly. "I'm not sorry. Are you?"

"No." He paused. "I wish like hell you weren't Peter's girl...."

"I'm *not*! Why do you keep bringing *Peter* into this?"

"Because he's there, damn it!" Patrick growled, surging to his feet.

"Weren't you the one who said Lance didn't exist anymore? Weren't you the one who said there were no memories to fight?"

"Then it looks like I was wrong," Patrick muttered, raking a hand through his hair in frustration. "I lived in Peter Kirkland's shadow for years and I'll be damned if I'll take his castoffs." Turning on his heel, he stormed off, not toward the shelter but into the woods.

Mouth agape, Jordanna stared at his vanishing form. Only when night had swallowed him completely did she clamp her mouth shut. Her trembling limbs spoke of her fury, her wide eyes broadcast hurt. Oh, she was no novice to cutting statements, but coming from this man and on the tail of his spectacular kiss...it stung.

The worst was that he was gone, and there was absolutely nothing she could do by way of reply. She felt frustrated, impotent. She'd been wronged and was helpless to correct the situation.

As the quiet minutes passed, she cooled down, but the hurt lingered long after she'd returned to the shelter. When she finally fell asleep it was nearly dawn. Patrick had not returned.

"JORDANNA?"

A gentle hand shook her shoulder, then tentatively rubbed her back.

"Wake up, Jordanna."

She heard his voice from far away and pulled the sleeping bag more tightly over her head. It was too early, pitch-black, and she was tired, so tired.

"Come on, Jordanna. Everyone else is eating breakfast."

She slitted open an eye and searched the darkness, saw nothing, attributed the voice to a dream. Then she realized where she was. And remembered what had happened. On pure reflex, she recoiled from the hand on her shoulder and sat up, slowly lowering the sleeping bag to her shoulders.

To her chagrin, the sun was shining, which was unfair when she felt tired, disgruntled and stiff. Sure enough, the men were grouped around the small camp stove. She squinted at them, hoping Patrick would simply evaporate. When he remained squatting by her side, she turned to glare at him.

"You can leave now," she said coolly, clutching the sleeping bag to her breasts. "I'm awake." Twisting away, she dug a hairbrush from her pack.

"Jordanna?"

Her hand hovered, fingers gripping the brush handle.

"Look at me, Jordanna."

Very slowly she turned her head, her face a mask of tension.

"I'm sorry for what I said last night. It was wrong of me."

"You meant it. Why apologize?"

"I didn't mean to imply that you were one of Peter's castoffs."

"Then why did you say it?"

Looking down, he snapped a dried twig between

the fingers of one hand. "I was feeling threatened. I lashed out. It was juvenile." He sought her gaze again. "And cruel."

"You're right. It was both of those things, plus another—it was *wrong*." Eyes flashing, she stared him down. "I was the one who divorced Peter, not the other way around. I was the one who was fed up, who wanted out, who wanted something more than he had to offer. I cast *Peter* off, if you want to know the truth." She grew more skeptical. "And whatever would you have to feel threatened about?"

His eyes were a deep, deep brown that invited drowning. "You. The pleasure I felt when I kissed you."

Fighting his appeal, Jordanna looked away and briskly worked the brush through her hair. "It was just a kiss. Nothing threatening about it."

Strong fingers seized her chin and turned her face his way. "It was a *super* kiss. Don't tell me you didn't think so."

She felt positively belligerent. "Of course it was a super kiss. You're a pro, Lance. But it was *only* a kiss. Nothing to be threatened by." She was goading him without remorse. "Now, will you please let go of me?"

Patrick's features darkened. Very slowly he dropped his hand. "I hurt you, Jordanna, and I'm very sorry for that. If lashing back at me makes you feel better, go ahead." He sighed on a note of what Jordanna almost thought to be defeat. "You can use the stream to wash up and change. I'll keep the guys here for a while so you can have some privacy." Pushing himself to his feet, he turned and headed toward the others.

Determined to let him go his way, Jordanna busied herself with digging everything she'd need from her pack. Under cover of her sleeping bag, she tugged on yesterday's running suit, then, as Patrick had suggested, headed for the stream to clean up and put on the fresh things she carried.

The air was cold, the stream a challenge. Holding her breath, then expelling it in involuntary little cries, she threw handful after handful of water on her face. The diversion was welcome. By the time she'd dried and moisturized her skin, sponged off her body and gotten dressed again, she was tingling all over. And confused.

She ate breakfast quickly, packed up her things and set out with the others, all the while wondering why she wasn't furious with Patrick. She should be, she told herself. But she wasn't. Hurt as she'd been by the insult he'd hurled in the dark of the woods last night, she did believe that he was sorry. His apology had been forthright, his manner sincere. And he was obviously as bothered by the past as she was. Knowing well the arrogance of Peter Kirkland, she could begin to understand the bitter pill Patrick had had to swallow for years. She could begin to understand—and forgive—and that confused her all the more.

As though made to order, the day's route was demanding in terms both of strength and concentration. Once the group was twenty minutes into the hike, Jordanna's legs weren't the only ones to protest.

"Whew," John breathed, calling to Patrick from the end of the line. "Is it uphill all the way?"

Patrick looked back with a knowing smirk. "For a while. Problems?"

"Nope! Nope!"

"Why're you huffing and puffing like an old man?" Donald teased, directing his words to John, though catching Jordanna's eye and winking at her in a show of friendliness that surprised her. "*We're* all doin' fine."

"Speak for yourself, Don," Larry groaned, collapsing onto a rock and tugging at his boot. "I think yesterday's blister just woke up."

Patiently Patrick helped him put moleskin on the offended spot. "We'll take it slow," he avowed as they started off again. "But you'll earn your stripes today."

Jordanna was grateful. Unsure as to how to act with Patrick, she welcomed the hard work he drew from them all. As the morning progressed, they followed the Black Angel Trail to Rim Junction, where five different trails met in an intersection as confusing as any Jordanna had ever seen. There were no street signs, no service stations or churches or McDonalds to distinguish one trail from the next.

But Patrick knew. At his direction they headed south onto the Basin Rim Trail. It was this trail that took them through stands of spruce and across ledges to the foot of Mount Meader.

"Doesn't look so tough," Bill observed, eyeing the wooded crest when they were still a distance away.

"Gettin' bigger," Donald commented sometime later.

"Man, this looks rugged," was John's accurate summation when they began the ascent.

It was rugged. Many of the rocky inclines called for teamwork in the scaling; packs were passed from hand to hand, freeing bodies to concentrate on handholds and steady footing. To Jordanna's relief, Patrick kept his distance, seeming determined to let her hack it on her own. And she did. Ignoring muscles that clamored for a rest, she kept pace with the men through the steep climb. By the time they stopped for lunch on the scenic lookout ledges near the summit, though, she was grateful to crumple on a rock and lie back against her pack.

She wasn't the only one. Four men collapsed on the ledges nearby. Only Patrick had the strength to move around from pack to pack, gathering and distributing Slim Jims, Triscuits and nuts.

"Is this exhilaration?" Larry asked, doubt written all over his pale face.

"Sure," Bill said, reaching for the plastic container of peanut butter Patrick offered. "You're just out of shape. I told you to build yourself up before you came."

"I did. I did."

"How many knee bends?" Donald asked, squirting a blob of jelly from a plastic tube.

"Enough," Larry mumbled.

As always, Jordanna was slightly apart from the others. Patrick sank to the ground by her side. "You're doin' fine," he observed casually.

"It's fun," she replied cautiously.

"Not mad at me anymore?"

She thought for a minute. "I think I walked it off."

"That's good."

Unwrapping a Slim Jim, she bit off a piece. "I like the exertion."

"Not tired?"

"I didn't say *that*." After listening to the men's talk with half an ear, she spoke again. It was time she explained herself. "Backpacking is an adventure I've never had the opportunity to take part in before. When Craig called, the time seemed right. Things were only mildly chaotic at the office for a change. I needed a vacation. Winter will set in before long, and I'll be stuck inside."

"You don't ski?"

"No. Do you?"

His lips twitched. "I tried. I wasn't too good at it."

"A professional athlete? I can't believe that."

His eyes went cold for an instant. "I *was* a professional athlete. Past tense. And being good at one sport doesn't imply skill at all others."

"I didn't mean that," she said softly, then corrected herself. "Well, maybe I did. You were supercoordinated on the field. You're a pro here in the hills. I guess I assumed...well, I'm sorry. I didn't realize you were sensitive."

He popped a cashew into his mouth. "I'm tired. That's all. It was bad enough in my playing days having to constantly compete with...the other talent on the field. Now people expect me to compete with the man I was then." He raised his eyes to hers. No longer cold, they were nonetheless earnest. "I can't. I don't want to." As though unconsciously punctuating his words, he flexed his shoulder, rubbed it, then dropped another nut into his mouth.

"Does it hurt?"

"Not competing?"

"I was thinking of your shoulder, but I guess the question could apply to that too."

"Both. On occasion."

"Does your pack bother it? Your shoulder, that is."

He crinkled his nose, looking almost boyish. "Nah. Well, maybe once in a while. It's okay."

Again they sat in silence, taking their turns with the peanut butter and jelly, then the Tang. Jordanna found herself thinking of what he'd said and feeling touched by what appeared to be nicks in his armor. Peter had had no nicks. He'd been perfect. Bright and shining. Invincible. And, as time had passed, totally obnoxious.

"What do you do?" she asked, searching for fodder to further delineate Patrick from his archrival. When he looked up questioningly, she gestured broadly. "Job-type thing."

He hesitated for a minute. "What do *you* think I do?"

The sudden twinkle in his eye evoked even greater indulgence on her part. "Oh, no. You're not getting me into trouble with that one."

"Come on," he coaxed, seeming fully at ease. "If you were to imagine what a football-playing has-been would do, what would it be?"

Ironic she mused, how he could still feel such bitterness toward Peter, yet toward his career's demise, none at all. It gave her courage. "When I first saw you yesterday, I wondered if you were either coaching or broadcasting. But you're so determined that the days of the Lance are over that I'd have to rule those out. Which also rules out the probability of living off endorsements." As Peter did, she was going to say, but prudently caught herself. Her eyes narrowed on Patrick in speculation. "You could be selling cars or clothes or real estate." She arched a brow. "Some former greats own restaurant chains." Her gaze fell to the remains of the Slim Jim in her hand, then skipped to the Triscuit Patrick was about to dunk in the peanut-butter tub. Gourmet fare? "Forget that. No restaurants."

He chuckled. "No restaurants. Try again."

"You're very good with people," she reflected as her gaze encompassed the men nearby. "Management? Personnel? Wait. I'll bet you're a psychology professor."

"You were closer before," he said softly. "I'm in business."

"Oh?"

He nodded. "Venture capitalism."

"Oh."

He laughed aloud at her comical change of expression. "What's wrong with being a venture capitalist?"

She scowled. "Nothing. I suppose."

"Come on. Out with it."

She took a breath. "I went to a bunch of investors when I was first setting up the business. They turned me down cold."

"Maybe they didn't think you could make it."

"Obviously." She gave a sly smile. "They must be choking on their Scotch now."

"We don't *all* drink Scotch...."

"True," she admitted, realizing she probably sounded as bigoted as those she accused. Relenting, she shrugged. "You must do some good."

"I think so. In the six years my group's been at it, we've set up several dozen new businesses and put any number of others back on their feet from states of near bankruptcy."

"Have any of those businesses been women-run?" she asked skeptically.

"Several." His eyes held meaning. "We don't discriminate. If a woman's got it all together, we'll take her on."

"Your investors agree?"

"They trust us."

"I see."

"Come to think of it, we've never gone wrong with a woman. Those few disasters we've had have been male-run all the way."

"Perhaps there's a double standard at play," Jordanna mused, unable to help herself. "Women have to work twice as hard. They have to be twice as good. Isn't it possible that to be accepted by your group she's got to be far superior to everyone else out there?"

Patrick was undaunted by her not-so-subtle accusation. "I'd like to think that *anyone* we decide to back is far superior to the rest of the field. It's my money and my partners' *and* that of the investors we corral to join us. But—'' he gestured dismissively ''—it's not only the money we put up. It's the working together. The management. That's where the real challenge comes in.''

She eyed him warily. ''It does excite you, doesn't it?''

''Yes.''

''And I suppose you do it well.''

''I hope so. I'd like to believe that much is part of my personality,'' he said gently. ''It's the competitive instinct. Football or business—I wouldn't do it at all if I couldn't do it well.''

Nodding, she sat back to munch on the cashews he handed her. A fast glance at the other men was enough to assure her that she and Patrick had privacy of sorts. ''You've never married?''

''The same theory applies. I refuse to do it if I can't do it well.'' He gave a lopsided grin. ''I've never found the woman who, shall we say, inspired that forever instinct.'' Shifting and stretching out on the ground, he pillowed his head with his hands and closed his eyes.

Jordanna's gaze raked his supine form. Long, well-formed legs lay beneath denim made soft and supple by wear. The broad chest she'd so admired pulled his navy turtleneck taut; both were framed by the open zipper of his Goretex shell. His cheeks were lean and clean shaven, a far cry from the day's stubble sported by the four other men. His hair was thick and full, clipped close only at the sideburns and neck. Long, dark lashes dusted cheekbones that were high, strong and tanned.

Clamping her eyes shut against the involuntary flutter in her middle, she slowly settled onto her back to follow his lead and absorb the sun's warm noontime rays. Only with the passage of several moments did she open one eye to steal another look.

Patrick was waiting for her. He rolled to his stomach, bringing himself within inches of her. "I wondered if you were falling asleep," he murmured. "You look tired."

Tipping her head more fully his way, she opened the other eye. "I seem to have had a minimum of sleep the past two nights."

"Two? Then there was a wild farewell Sunday night with a special someone?"

Her smile was soft. "Not quite. I was up late cramming for this trip."

"Cramming?"

"Reading everything I could about backpacking. Thank heavens for bookstores open on Sundays."

He returned her smile with one that was heart-stoppingly gentle. "You're quite something, ya know that?"

"Not really," she said, and meant it. Though she was proud of what she'd made of her life, she was far from cocky. And she'd never before found a man confident enough to compliment her with such honest admiration.

"You're blushing. It's pretty." At his whisper-soft words her color rose all the more. "You've aged beautifully, Jordanna. I swear you look even better than you did when you were with Peter, and you were gorgeous then. How old are you? Thirty? Thirty-one?"

Enjoying his attention, she propped her ear on her palm. "Thirty-two."

"You married young."

"I was nineteen and dumb." Her grin took the sting from her words. Patrick lifted a finger to trace its soft curve.

"Funny, our meeting this way...you and I, away from all that...."

She nipped at the tip of his finger. "It is funny."

"You're a great kisser."

"So are you."

His lips twitched playfully. "But it'd be *really* dumb if we got involved with each other."

Her eyes glowed a seductive amber-in-hazel. "*I'll* say."

"How about a fling? You know, a three-night stand with sleeping bags zipped together?"

She winced and hoarsely whispered his name, drawing out both syllables. "Pat-rick! With *them*?" The grimace she tossed toward the others was comical.

"Of course not," he whispered back. "I could drag you by the hair into the woods—"

"Caveman tactics, hmm?"

"If need be. You turn me on, Jordanna."

"The feeling's mutual."

"But dumb."

"Really dumb."

He sighed then, a long, slightly wavering exercise of the lungs. "We'll have to try to remember that," he croaked. Then he cleared his throat, pushed himself up and raised his voice to call to the others. "Okay. Let's clean up this mess and get going. As the man said, we've got miles to go before we sleep...."

THE AFTERNOON'S TREK was as rugged as the morning's. With much panting they reached the summit of Mount Meader, then wound down along the Meader Ridge Trail. One spectacular view followed the next—narrow ridges playing up distant mountain ranges, contortions of rock where long-gone glaciers had carved out the landscape, spruce-covered hillsides, craggy ravines. Larry had a field day with his camera. The others enjoyed each pause to make mental pictures of the sights.

Seeming to have accepted her presence, the men included Jordanna in their talk from time to time. She came to realize that complaining was part of their fun. In truth they enjoyed the hike and its views as much as she did.

On the more tedious stretches of the trail, they walked in silence. Part of the path was boggy. Much of it now was downhill. As a runner, Jordanna knew the perils of the downhill trek. When Larry and Donald in tandem cursed their quads, she smiled knowingly.

They stopped for a break in the middle of the afternoon, then followed an old logging road through a forest of white birch. At last they reached Wild River.

"This is it?" Bill gawked in dismay.

Jordanna joined the men to stare at the dark bed of mossy rocks. "It is wild, isn't it?" she quipped, surprising herself with her own good humor when her shoulders, her back, her legs ached.

"We're upstream from the water," Patrick explained. "Come on. Campsite's not too far ahead."

By the time they reached the dry, flat area he had in mind, Jordanna was as happy as the others to shed her pack for the night. There was no formal shelter this time, simply an abundance of woods surrounding an open area with a rough circle of stones for a fire.

As had happened the day before when the sun set, the air grew rapidly cold. Sweat that had gathered during the trek dried. Jackets were momentarily shed for the donning of additional layers beneath.

Under Patrick's patient tutelage, the tents they'd carried were unfurled, erected and anchored. As Jordanna did her share of the work, so she did her share of speculation. Three two-man tents. Interesting. By the time she stood admiring one such finished product, the other two tents were spoken for. She looked at Patrick. He looked at her. Then, with mirrored shrugs and the faintest tugging of smiles, they tossed their packs to the front of the one remaining tent and turned with relish to the prospect of a hot dinner.

As had happened the night before, Jordanna's eyelids began to droop long before she finished the coffee in her mug. The men had begun to play poker. Excusing herself as unobtrusively as she could, she crawled into the tent, stripped down to her long underwear, climbed into her sleeping bag and fell promptly asleep.

This time it wasn't snoring that woke her, but a pair of warm male lips caressing her brow.

3

THE SENSATION WAS PLEASURABLE, one of a delicious warmth in contrast to the cold night air. For long moments Jordanna succumbed to its allure, smiling in the state of half sleep from which she had no desire to emerge. She didn't want to think, didn't want to analyze the source of such simple bliss. Wakefulness was her enemy. But it could only be held off so long.

"Patrick," she murmured sleepily, "what are you doing?"

"Warming my lips," he breathed against her eyes. "It's damn cold out there."

"Not much better in here. My nose is freezing."

Instantly his warmth touched the afflicted feature. "Better?" he whispered, his breath coffee scented and very, very close.

Her eyelids flickered. Withdrawing a hand from its shelter deep inside her sleeping bag, she felt for his jaw. It moved slowly beneath her palm as he breathed soft kisses from the tip of her nose to its bridge.

"Funny, you don't feel cold," she mumbled, her grogginess dissipating by the second. His cheek was warm, as was his brow and, her fingers discovered when they slid into the thickness of his hair, his scalp. Moreover, his very nearness sent a wild shaft of heat through her body.

Suddenly she was wide awake...and aware of the folly of letting him kiss her further. Clutching a handful of his hair, she drew his head back. "Isn't there a law against this?"

"Against what?" he asked, his low voice the embodiment of innocence.

"Messing with the clientele."

"I love messing with the clientele."

Her fingers tightened. "You do this *all the time*?"

He twisted his head to alleviate the pain of her grip. "Ahh. Ease up." When she did, he rubbed the offended spot and spoke gruffly. "Of course I don't. What do you take me for?"

"I could take you for the same kind of rutting stallion Peter was," she said without thinking, then regretted it moments later when Patrick came down full length on top of her, pinning her body to the ground, her hand to the corner of the sleeping bag by her shoulder.

"I'm not Peter, Jordanna," he said in a dangerously low voice, then repeated it again very slowly and with feeling. "I'm not Peter. We may have shared a profession, a playing field on occasion, a podium from time to time and any amount of newsprint, but that's where the association ends." His grip tightened on her wrist. Even in the dark his eyes held hers, which were wide and stunned by the force of his reaction to her careless barb. "I don't know what kind of husband he was, or lover, and I don't give a damn. I do know that he was loud and brash and had a corner on the market for conceit—"

"Hey!" A muffled shout from without broke into his harangue. "What's going on over there!"

It was joined by a second, aimed snidely at the first. "What do you *think*'s going on?"

And a third, more indulgently. "They're talking football. Let them be."

"But I'm trying to sleep," complained the first.

"Could've fooled me," grumbled his tent mate. "You've been thrashing all over the—"

"Damn tent's too small!"

"Shut up, all of you," came the fourth, last but not least. "You're making more noise than the lovers!"

Jordanna could contain herself no longer. "Lovers?" she cried indignantly. "*Lovers?* Are you all mad?"

Patrick's fingers sealed her lips as he raised his head to address the shrouded night. "You guys better get some sleep. Jordanna and I just had a minor disagreement. We'll keep it down."

There were several vague grunts, followed by silence. Jordanna held her breath, abundantly aware of Patrick's hard length pressing her to the ground. Even the padding of her sleeping bag seemed insignificant against his commanding form. She had mixed feelings when he rolled onto his back atop his own sleeping bag.

The silence was thick, the tent suddenly minuscule. Jordanna listened to the sound of Patrick's breathing and wondered what had happened to those other sounds of the night. There seemed no breeze, no stirring of woodland creatures across the carpet of dried leaves, no distant trickle of the stream. Only Patrick. Breathing far more steadily, she cursed silently, than was she.

Unable to stand the kind of suspense that hung in the air, she turned her head in his direction. "Pat?" she whispered.

When at last he gave a quiet, "Mmm?", she breathed a sigh of relief. She knew he wasn't asleep, but she wasn't sure whether he'd admit it.

"Pat, I'm sorry." The simplest part of what she had to say came fast. Now she began to struggle for the right words. "I...well...I didn't mean to compare you with Peter. It...it kind of came out all by itself." She looked toward the roof of the tent, then threw an arm across her eyes. When Patrick remained silent, she realized he wasn't going to help her. She stumbled on. "I really...I really haven't been with that many men. I mean, I don't sleep around and I guess you make me...feel vulnerable...." She swore softly and turned onto her side away from him. Scowling into the darkness, she wondered how she'd managed to make such a mess of something so small. What had he said—that he loved messing with the clientele? Of course he'd been teasing her. Of course?

"I was only teasing," he whispered as if on cue. With a sudden movement, he reached out and slid an arm beneath her to roll her back toward him. Jordanna's initial resistance owed more to the strangeness of the intimacy than to genuine reluctance; after several seconds, she relaxed against his supine form, letting her cheek rest in the crook of his shoulder while his arm held her fast. "Not all men bed-hop, Jordanna. There are those of us who are somewhat fastidious. It's as intimate, as private, as special an act for me as it is for you, you know."

She hadn't thought about it that way and now that she did, particularly hearing the words on Patrick's lips, she felt a shimmer of electricity sear her in passing. In part to fight that unbidden awareness, she resorted to gentle mockery. "Are you trying to tell me you're a virgin?"

His chuckle was priceless and worth the risk she'd taken that his good humor had returned. "Not quite. But I don't sleep around either. I may never have married, but I've been lucky enough to have had some truly fine relationships with women. I've learned from them. I've learned a lot." He slanted his head down; his lips brushed her brow as he spoke. "Among other things, I've learned that respect is critical to any meaningful relationship. Self-respect, as well as respect for one's partner. No, Jordanna, I don't mess around with the clientele." His already low voice dropped to a nearly inaudible level. "At least, I never have before...."

"I heard that," Jordanna whispered through a gentle smile. "And thank you for saying it. It's a relief to know that I'm not the only one acting out of character."

Again came the chuckle that tickled her pink. "Not by a long shot, angel." His arm tightened momentarily around her. "Must be something about this backwoods air that plays havoc with the hormones."

"Guess so," she murmured softly, then moved her hand along his chest. Above the waist, he wore nothing more than a thermal shirt like hers, but she was further bundled in her sleeping bag. "You must be freezing!" she exclaimed, moving her hand in a larger arc. "Don't you want to get into your sleeping bag?"

"Not...particularly."

"Why not?"

Again his breath played against her brow. "Because that'll be one more layer between us. *Your* sleeping bag's bad enough." Shifting deftly onto his side, he brought his face opposite hers. "Let's zip them together. Come on. What do you say?"

Jordanna's shiver was not from the cold. "I say that we'd be crazy to do that."

"We'd be warm."

"Too warm."

"Listen," he began, reaching out through the darkness to stroke her hair with an ease that belied the urgency in his voice, "I know you're not loose. And I know I'm not either. But, damn it, something's happening here. I take one look at you and—bam—I forget who we are, where we are, and the only thing I want to do is to take you in my arms and...."

"And?"

"Make love to you."

Jordanna's insides quivered. She couldn't deny anything Patrick said, for her body clamored likewise. Unable to help herself, she placed her fingers against his lips, ostensibly stilling him while in reality very slowly exploring his lips in the way of the blind. "You shouldn't say things like that, Pat. They're nearly irresistible."

"They're meant to be," he whispered without remorse. "So, how about it? Should we warm each other?"

"No."

"Mmm." With a soulful sigh, he released her. "Dumb."

"Uh-huh."

For long moments they lay in silence. Finally, Patrick raised himself enough to slide into his sleeping bag. It seemed forever until he made himself comfortable and lay still. "Damn tent," he muttered, squirming again. "Whose brilliant idea was it to sleep here?"

"Yours."

He cleared his throat. "Right."

Again they said nothing for a stretch. Jordanna was so acutely aware of the body next to hers that she had to concentrate on breathing steadily. Patrick turned away onto his side, lay there for several minutes, then flipped back.

"I can't sleep," he announced, sounding so much like a little boy that Jordanna couldn't help but laugh.

"Of course you can't. You must be running plays over and over in your mind."

"I am not running plays."

"Then why don't you try lying still?"

"I'm trying. I'm trying. It's all your fault, you know."

"*My* fault?"

"I can't sleep with you lying so close."

"What would you like me to do? Move outside."

"No. Move over."

"There's no room!"

"That's the point." Suddenly he was up on an elbow. Though Jordanna couldn't see a thing in the dark, she felt his every move. "How about a goodnight kiss."

She tipped her head his way. "What good'll *that* do?"

"It'll settle me down."

She laughed again. "I think your reasoning's screwed up."

"No, no," he returned earnestly. "I keep wondering if it'll be as good the second time round. If it's not, I'll be cured."

"And if it is? Then what?"

"Maybe I'll get it out of my system."

"You're a dreamer, Patrick Clayes."

He thought about that for a minute. "Mmm. I suppose so. How about you? Do you dream?"

"On occasion."

"About what?"

"Now you're really getting personal."

"Come on. Tell me. What do you dream about?"

"Work. Success."

"And...?"

"That's it," she lied. "Very simple."

"Very dry. Very boring. Surely you fantasize. About men. Love. Sex."

"Do you?"

"About men? Not quite. About love and sex? All the time."

"Tell me," she coaxed, turning the tables. "What are your greatest fantasies?"

"Oh, I dream about a woman, *the* woman."

"What does she look like?"

"I don't know," he murmured. "It's not her looks that make her so special. It's her warmth. Her individuality. Her caring. That's it. Her caring. She cares for me above and beyond anything and everything else in life."

"A pretty self-centered fantasy, isn't it?"

"Hell, no. I care for her the same way. It's just that, well, I've never really had anyone who cared for me that much... and it matters."

"What about your parents? Surely they loved you."

"Oh, yeah. They did. Me and my four brothers and three sisters."

"Eight kids? Wow, that's great!"

"Not when you want that little bit of individual attention. I was the baby. My older siblings were stuck looking after me more often than not. And I do mean *stuck*. They weren't terribly thrilled about having a constant tagalong. When I took to playing football, we were all relieved."

"You started playing young?"

"I was seven when I began tackling kids on the street. I began throwing the ball a year later. When I was nine I joined a peewee league. You know the rest."

But she hadn't known the first, and it was enlightening, to say the least. It certainly explained his drive, not to mention the frustration he must have felt coming in second to Peter Kirkland all those years.

"Your parents must have been proud of what you made of yourself."

"I suppose. But we were never close. I resented them for years."

"Do you still?"

"They're dead."

"Oh, Pat, I'm sorry."

He paused then, growing more pensive. "I am too. It took a lot of growing up for me to begin to understand that they did what they had to do." His voice hardened. "But I'll never do that to a kid of mine. I want two kids. That's all. And I'll give them everything I've got."

"You'll spoil them rotten."

His laugh was gentle once more. "Which is why I need a good woman to keep me in line. So, angel, how about it?"

"How about what?"

"That good-night kiss," he whispered from close by her lips. "Now that I've spilled my gut, you owe me."

"Why do I feel I've been manipulated?" she returned, her breath suddenly in short supply.

"Not yet. If you want—" he curved his fingers around her shoulder and turned her toward him "—I'd be glad to comply."

"Patrick..." she whispered in warning.

"Just a kiss. One kiss." Without awaiting her reply, he closed the tiny distance between them, molding his mouth to hers as his arms completed a circle of her back and drew her on top of him.

Jordanna simply couldn't resist his virile call. She found him far too attractive to begin with and, now that he'd let her into his private domain, felt all the more drawn to him. For the moment it didn't matter that he'd been Peter's rival all those years, or that there were four men within easy hearing distance. The tent was their shield, the night further fortification. She gave herself up to his kiss because he touched something raw within her, something that all the protestation in the world couldn't deny.

His lips opened searingly over hers, caressing her warmth, partaking of her essence. Again and again he drank of her, draining her until the thirst was mutual and acute. His tongue thrust deeply, scorching hers, matching its length, then drawing it into his own mouth. When his arms left her back to frame her face, she bolstered herself on her palms. Only then did his lips release hers to lie half open against her cheek.

"Well...?" she whispered tremulously.

"Better than the first. I think...we're in...trouble." The slight adjustment he made in the positioning of his hips elaborated on the problem.

"I think I'd better get back on my side of the tent," she mumbled, but when she made to do so, he slipped his hands beneath her arms and held her still.

"No. Not yet."

"We've been over this before, Pat. It's not sane."

"But it sure feels good," he rasped, then took her mouth again with the sureness of a magnet drawn to its kind. And Jordanna was helpless, riveted to him by the seeking spirals of desire curling through her veins. "Tell me it doesn't," he dared, when at last he came up for a breath.

"It does. It does," she cried. "But that's not the point."

"You're damn right," he said with another meaningful shift of his hips. "It's lower and deeper and—"

"Shh!" She brought a hand to his mouth, then gasped when his own took advantage of her move and slid to encircle her breast.

He moaned softly. "Oh, God, Jordanna. You're so firm. So full." His hand gently kneaded her, his thumb finding then teasing the tautness of her nipple.

She sucked in a deeper breath and, closing her eyes, arched her back. Her one supporting arm trembled, but she could no more have removed herself from him than she could have denied, at that moment, the very obvious proof of her arousal.

"Come here," he growled, hauling her higher until his lips touched the fullness of her breast. Through the fabric of her shirt he nibbled at her flesh. His tongue dampened the thermal cloth, sending a fiery heat through her skin toward her most feminine core.

Lost in a world of exquisite pleasure, Jordanna sighed his name. She lowered her head and buried her face in his hair, breathing deeply of its clean male scent. Through vague remnants of lucidity, she wondered how anyone could smell so clean after traipsing through the woods for the better part of two days, then realized that what struck her senses was the sheer maleness of Patrick Clayes. Chemistrywise, he could do no wrong.

Intentionwise, not so. Suddenly, he was a whirlwind of action, setting her down on her back and fighting with the darkness for something she couldn't fathom.

"What are you *doing*?" she gasped, twisting as his hands searched on either side of her.

"The damn sleeping bag's in the way," he growled, sitting up and continuing his struggle. "We've got to get them together—"

Miraculously she found his hands and anchored them to her chest. "No!" she cried, then lowered her voice to a husky whisper. "No, Pat. Please. Don't."

He was breathing heavily. She all but felt the ragged rise and fall of his chest a foot above her. "Why not? You felt what I did."

"But it's wrong," she went on breathlessly, holding his hands all the more tightly, fearful of what might happen should he touch her again. "It's wrong. We have too much to fight, you and I. You heard the guys before. They said we were talking football. Well, we were, in a way. Your past *is* football. So is mine, in a sense. The only difference is that where football for you was a saving grace, for me it was hell. Pure hell."

Though his hands remained coiled steel in hers, Patrick went very still. "You've got to be kidding."

"Oh, no, I'm not. That game—"

"Not about football," he snapped. "About stopping."

"That too," she whispered on a breath of despair.

"Good Lord, do you have any idea—"

The sharp squeeze she gave his hands stilled his words. "I do. I know what you feel. And I'd be lying if I said I didn't feel the same. Frustration isn't a man's prerogative, y'know." When he fell back onto his sleeping bag, she released his hands.

"Ah, hell. Another lecture on sexism."

Jordanna stiffened, curling her now empty fingers into the material of her sleeping bag. "I don't give lectures on sexism. I state facts."

"Well, so do I," Patrick countered, rearing up once more and leaning close. "And the facts are, one, that I need you, and, two, that you need me."

"You've forgotten several others," she stated in a pained voice. "Three, neither of us goes in for casual affairs. Four, we've got to be able to live with ourselves in the morning. Five, we have another three days of trekking through the woods with a group of men who'll make the most out of any relationship we have. And six, come Friday night we go our separate ways." She lowered her voice. "Not to mention the facts that, seven, I'm Peter Kirkland's ex-wife and you're through with taking seconds, and, eight, that I've had my fill of athletic egotists.''

She stopped then, breathless and spent. Patrick was as speechless.

When at last he spoke, his words were preceded by a weary sigh. ''Well, I guess you've covered everything. Good night, Jordanna.'' Turning away from her, he lay perfectly still.

It took Jordanna far longer to quiet her rampaging nerves.

WEDNESDAY MORNING dawned bleak and overcast, a fitting backdrop to Jordanna's mood. Awakening to find herself alone in the tent, she snatched up her things and headed for the stream. She was relieved to find the campsite quiet. The last thing she needed was a smart comment from one of the men about something that might have been overheard in the night.

Head down, brows drawn together, she distractedly followed the path. When she reached the edge of the stream, she put down her things, then straightened, moaning aloud when the muscles of her back protested the simple movement.

''What's wrong, Jordanna?'' came a deep voice from the side. ''Feeling stiff?''

Her gaze spun to focus on Patrick, who leaned indolently against the peeling trunk of a tall birch. ''Playing Peeping Tom today?'' she snapped, to cover her surprise. Not that she shouldn't have guessed he might be here. After all, he hadn't been in the tent, and he hadn't been in the campsite's clearing.

He stood his ground, holding her gaze. ''Just answering nature's call,'' he announced bluntly. ''What's your excuse?''

''I might say the same, but I guess it'll have to wait.'' Turning back to the stream, she knelt, gingerly submerged her hands in the cold water, then pressed them to her face.

"Not a morning person, I gather?" he asked, from closer this time. When Jordanna didn't answer but simply kept her cold fingers pressed to her eyes, he spoke again, more gently this time. "If it's any solace, I've just walked off some of my own black mood. I didn't think anyone else would be up this early."

"What time is it?" she murmured, dipping her hands in the water again and reapplying them to her face.

"Seven."

She moaned softly. "Must be force of habit...." She quickly splashed her face several times in succession, gasped against the cold, then reached to the side and pressed her towel to her face. When firm hands began a gentle massage of her shoulders, she stiffened only momentarily before relaxing under the patient ministration.

"That's it," he coaxed softly. "That's it. Just let go."

With a shuddering breath, she dropped her head back, then forward again. "I'm so tired," she murmured, any annoyance she might have felt toward Patrick forgotten as his deft thumbs kneaded the taut lines of her neck.

"You've kept right up with the rest. You should feel proud of that."

"But I'm so tired. I swear I could sleep for a week."

"All you need is a good night's rest. That's three in a row now without, hmm?"

"Mmm."

From his haunches, Patrick slid his knees to the ground and eased Jordanna back into the cradle of his thighs. His mouth was by her temple, his arms overlapping below her breasts. "The soreness will wear off once we get going. It always does."

"I don't know. The thought of lifting that pack doesn't thrill me."

"I could take some of your load."

"And let the others think I'm giving in? No way."

"You know, you can only fight being a woman up to a point. It's a biological fact that a woman's body has a lower proportion of muscle than a man's. It'd be only natural if you—"

"I'm okay," she asserted, but made no move to withdraw from the comfortable haven he offered. It was the most welcome support she'd had in days.

Patrick slid his cheek against her hair. "You're an enigma to me, Jordanna. Do you know that?"

"Me? An enigma? I thought I was pretty straightforward."

"That's part of the fascination. You're so in command at times, then at other times, like now, so much more vulnerable. I don't think I've known anyone with quite so many facets, and I get the strange feeling that I haven't seen half."

Her chuckle was soft and short. "Neither have I. I constantly surprise myself." Most surprising was the way she was yielding once again to Patrick's appeal.

"Tell me you like the theater."

"Living in Manhattan? Of course."

"And P. J. Clark's?"

"Hamburgers on paper plates with super steak fries and an occasional celebrity or two? You bet."

"And alfalfa sprouts?"

"Nice and crunchy. Sure."

"And the late, late show on TV?"

"As long as it's a two-tissue romance."

She had barely realized her confession when the snap and rustle of footsteps on the woodland floor heralded new arrivals.

"Oh, Lord," Donald moaned, but there was a teasing note to his voice, "they're still at it."

"And here we thought they'd be holed up in that tent for another hour at least," Larry quipped.

Coming to stand before the stream, John glanced down. "Guess we won't be throwing the water through the flap after all."

Neither releasing Jordanna nor looking up, Patrick grinned against her hair. "Try that, bud, and you're apt to find something wet and wriggly in your boot."

Jordanna withered into Patrick. "Oh, God, are there snakes around here?"

His response was flush by her ear. "None that you'll see. But I know where to look and if need be—"

"He's serious, guys," she called out loud and clear. "Better watch it with the water. For that matter, better watch it with the wisecracks. If he's offended, there's no telling what the man might do."

A groggy Bill emerged from the path and came to a standstill looking disgruntledly toward the duo by the stream. "What're *they* doing?"

"Come to think of it, we never did find out," John stated.

"What *are* you doing?" Larry asked more directly.

Jordanna dropped her gaze to the stream and in so doing missed the look of utter blankness on Patrick's face. "Doing? Us?" He squeezed her middle when she began to snicker. "Ah, we're... we're washing. That is, I was showing Jordanna how to wash." He lowered his voice in a conspiratorial manner. "You know how it is with city women. They're kind of slow—ah!" Jordanna's elbow caught him in the ribs. He released her as he would a hot potato and stood. "And ornery first thing in the morning. You guys can have 'er!" With that, he turned on his heel and headed back toward camp.

Taking his departure with good grace, Jordanna

reached for her tube of moisturizing cream. Though she would never have opted for an audience had she had a choice, pride held her rooted to the spot.

"Whaddya say, guys?" Bill asked good-naturedly. "Who wants her? John?"

"No, thanks. She's too good on the trail. I can barely keep up. My ego's taking a bruising."

"Larry?"

"Are you kidding? She probably earns twice what I do."

"Don?"

"Marie would kill me. Hey, how about you, wise guy? You're the only bachelor around here."

While Jordanna very placidly massaged moisturizer onto her face and hands, looking for all the world as though she were alone by the stream, Bill made pretense of mulling a possible purchase, narrowing his eyes, stroking his stubbled jaw. "I dunno. She is kinda pretty." Jordanna tipped her head to the side. "Nice neck. But she's awful skinny."

"The word is slender," Jordanna corrected with just the right amount of haughtiness, "and if I were five pounds heavier you'd probably be worrying about cellulite."

"Got a sharp tongue," Bill went on. "And she can't cook." He gestured dismissively. "Clayes can have her back. Not a bad match, actually. He cooks and cleans, she earns the money, and in their spare time they—"

"Talk football," John interjected propitiously. "They've got a lot in common." He shook his head. "Kirkland and Clayes...whew!"

Suddenly, Jordanna had heard enough. Gathering her things quickly together, she rose and headed for the path. "Thank you, gentlemen," she mocked on the move. "I can't remember when I've awoken to such clever repartee."

"But that was only the first act...!" Donald called after her.

Without missing a beat, she raised a hand. "I'm sure you'll enthrall one another with the second and third. What *I* need right about now is a strong cup of coffee."

It helped, as did the relative silence in which she was allowed to eat breakfast. Though the sky remained overcast, her mood slowly improved. She felt anger neither toward the men, whose earlier teasing had been without malice, nor toward Patrick, whose nocturnal ardor had been replaced by a more objective civility.

If he found her an enigma, she found him no different. But the confusion she felt regarding her feelings toward him were thrust to the back of her mind by the urgency of the day's activities.

With breakfast done, the tents disassembled and packs reloaded and donned, the troop set out on what was to be an easier trek than the day before had been. That was fortunate. Jordanna wasn't the only one whose body had felt the strain; her voice was but the softest in a chorus of furtive moans when Patrick led them upstream toward Eagle Link.

They stopped often, as much to admire the scenery as to pamper themselves. Jordanna found Patrick to be a wellspring of information regarding not only the history of the forest through which they passed but the wildlife and plant life as well. She wondered at the dedication behind such a store of knowledge; neither a football stadium nor a business office would have given him any of it. Then she remembered what he'd said about either doing things well or not doing them at all, and she surmised that somewhere in his library was a shelf or two filled with books on the great outdoors.

As the morning progressed, they moved slowly

along, joining the Wild River Trail, winding westward. More than once the sky darkened, but the threatening downpour held off. More than once Jordanna gave a sigh of relief.

"You've got rain gear, haven't you?" Patrick asked, catching one of her fearful glances skyward.

"Oh, yeah. I've got it. That doesn't mean I want to wear it."

He glanced at the wool sweater peering from the open neck of her jacket. "Are you warm enough?"

"Mmm. Pretty toasty."

His gaze dropped. "How about your feet? Those things don't look half as sturdy as my boots."

"These *things*," she returned with a half smile, "are phenomenally comfortable. *And* warm. I think I'll give them a good report. No blisters. No frostbite."

Patrick drew back an overhanging branch to allow them passage. "But if it rains? Will they keep you dry?"

"Well, uh, that's up for grabs." She frowned in annoyance. "It wasn't supposed to rain." Then she scrunched up her nose and sent him a pleading look. "Do you think it will?"

Patrick laughed aloud. "Your face. It's amazing."

"Will it rain?" she repeated, reluctant to get into a personal discussion.

He shrugged. "We'll see. In time.'

It didn't, though as a precaution, they munched on trail snacks of raisins and candies, saving lunch for early afternoon when they reached Perkins Notch, where they'd be spending the night. When, after lunch, Patrick set out to lead the men to Red Brook for trout fishing, Jordanna opted to stay behind.

"Are you sure you don't want to come?" Patrick asked quietly while the others gathered their reels and rods.

She gave a soft smile. "I'm sure. Fishing has never interested me."

"We're all going. You'll be here all alone."

"That's what I'm hoping," she quipped lightly, then took a deep breath and looked around the campsite. "I thought I'd take it easy. Maybe read. Maybe sleep. I could use the solitude." She arched her brows. "And the shelter, should it start to pour."

"Don't even think that," Patrick advised, chucking her on the chin and turning. "Be good," were his parting words as he loped off toward the others who were waiting. "We'll be back by sundown. Have the home fire waiting." There were several chuckles from the others as they moved off. Jordanna simply stood and looked after them until the path swallowed them up. Then, propping herself against the trunk of a gracious pine, she put her head back against its knobby spine and closed her eyes.

It was quiet. She needed that. A far cry from her midtown Manhattan office, she mused, wondering for the first time how things were going, whether everything was running smoothly in her absence, what emergencies might possibly arise and how they would be handled when she was, for all practical purposes, incommunicado.

Opening her eyes, she focused on the spot in the woods where Patrick had disappeared. He'd looked so hardy wearing his old faded jeans and boots, his wool jacket, his down vest. She liked him. That was part of the problem. She actually liked him.

Quite unbidden, the image of Peter Kirkland formed in her mind, reconstructing itself from the memories she'd so firmly tried to relegate to oblivion. She'd liked him too...at first. No, she'd loved him. She'd been smitten by his charm, his physique, his sheer charisma. Too late she'd learned that he'd been smitten by the very same things. Increasingly he'd believed in his own press as the months of their marriage had gone by.

It amazed her that she'd lasted three years. With a shudder she recalled the parties they'd gone to, she willingly at first, then with increasing reluctance when she'd found herself alone for much of the night with nothing to bolster her dignity but the fact that she was Peter Kirkland's wife. She was an appendage, nothing more. In time she'd begun to resent that fact.

Miraculously, given the cloistered nature of so much of her life, she'd grown. Or rather, she'd had time, and time aplenty, to analyze her existence and its shortcomings. She'd needed something to do, some identity of her own. Peter had not taken kindly to that conclusion.

"Are you crazy? You don't need to work. I make more than enough to support us. And I need you here. You're my wife."

"But I'm stagnating, Peter. You're off traveling half of the season. And when you're here you're either at practices or meetings or press conferences or...or...God only knows where." She'd begun to have her suspicions, but she'd kept them to herself. "I need something of my own. Something to sign *my* name to."

"Seems to me you sign your name to a whole load of charge cards."

"I'm bored! Can't you understand that?"

"Frankly," he'd returned with typical arrogance, "no. You've got me. You've got this house—"

"And what am I supposed to do? Clean all day? Spend hours preparing a gourmet meal, never knowing whether you'll come up with a last-minute meeting that you've just got to attend?"

His eyes had hardened then, taking on an ugly gleam. "Jordanna, you're being selfish. I'm the focal point of the team. I have to be there. You know that."

"No, I don't! If you're so important, you should be able to call the shots. Tell them your wife is waiting. Tell them you've got a prior engagement. Tell them to find someone else for a change."

"Someone else won't do. They want me. And I like it that way."

"I know," she'd muttered in defeat. "That's half of the problem. But what about me? What about *me*, Peter?"

"You can cook. You can clean. You can be waiting here for me when I get home. I'd think that would be enough."

"Well, it's not!"

He hadn't even heard her. "Besides, what would people think if my wife went out on her own? And what could you possibly do? You're not trained for anything—" he'd grinned smugly "—besides being my wife." He'd put his arm around her rigid shoulder. "Come on, honey. One superstar is enough for the two of us. Come here. Give a kiss."

Flinching in disgust, Jordanna snapped herself from the past. It was done. Over. Peter Kirkland had charmed her once too often, once too shallowly, once too condescendingly. He'd used her as he had his cleats, valuing them for one purpose and one purpose alone, and that was to make Peter Kirkland run faster. Somehow, she mused, she suspected he'd loved his cleats more....

And now there was Patrick. Every bit as good-looking. Nearly as successful. Little boys. That's what they were. Running into each other. Tripping over each other. Squeezing the life out of that poor, misshapen ball.

But she did like Patrick. She couldn't deny that fact. Much as she wanted to think him as egotistical as Peter, she couldn't. But then, what did she have to judge him on? Three days and two nights in the woods of New Hampshire? Okay, so he could cook. So he seemed more than willing to do it. Hell, he was the only one who knew how to work the portable stove!

Still, there were other things that puzzled her, not the least of which was his refusal to discuss football, his insistence that those days were over. While Peter was still milking his jock-high image for every penny it was worth, Patrick was off leading novice backpackers through the woods...when he wasn't in an office ferreting out new ventures to back.

Strange. It was strange. Too bad Patrick hadn't been the one she'd met when she'd been nineteen.

With a sigh, she pushed herself to her feet and, thrusting her hands in her pockets, wandered back along the trail they'd taken earlier, to No-Ketchum Pond. The land by the edge of the long, narrow pond was boggy, a floating mass of roots and moss she was careful to keep her distance from. No-Ketchum Pond. She smiled at the name and at Patrick's explanation of it, even as she prayed the men were having better luck with their fishing at Red Brook. The thought of fresh trout for dinner was infinitely appealing.

As was the thought of taking a nap, she decided with a yawn. Pulling her collar higher against her neck, she returned to the shelter, set her sleeping bag atop one of the board bunks, climbed in and closed her eyes. When next she opened them, it was dark and raining and she was still alone.

4

SLIPPING FROM HER SLEEPING BAG, Jordanna walked to the edge of the overhang and stared out at the pouring rain. Like the shelter they'd used Monday night, this one was enclosed on three sides. Here the fourth was partially fronted by the same weathered spruce logs as well. No tents tonight, she mused distractedly. At least she'd be spared that temptation... and its frustration.

Tucking her hands deep in her pockets, she pondered the gloom, then looked back toward her pack. She had a flashlight. No—the lantern. It was there, under cover of the eaves, perched beside the small stove, which Patrick had unpacked earlier. Kneeling quickly, she lit it, feeling vaguely reassured by its amber glow. Then she sat beside it, knees to her chest, waiting, waiting, for the men to return.

With each passing minute, she grew more concerned. Patrick had said they'd be back before dark. Yet it was dark *and* wet, and still there was no sign of humanity. Loath to imagine a mishap or worse, she directed her thoughts toward making something warm for the men's return. Could she light the stove? She eyed the small contraption. Any number of times now she'd watched Patrick light it. She knew that the first thing she had to do was to fill it with fuel lest they run out midmeal. It was easily done and she had a match in hand when she realized that she'd need water. Unfortunately, the source of pure water was not as convenient to the campsite as it had been on the past two nights.

Resigning herself to braving the rain, which was the least she could do given the soggy state the men would be in when they got back, she donned her rain suit, grabbed two pots and headed out. She'd barely left the campsite, though, when she stopped in her tracks, then returned to leave a note. He'd worry. She sensed it in her gut. And she didn't want that.

Replacing the small pad of paper and pen in her pack, she speared the note onto a corner of the stove within safe but visible distance from the lantern, then, hood up and flashlight in hand, set off again. Only after she'd doggedly struggled through the brush and reached the small spring Patrick had shown them earlier did she realize she might well have simply set the pots out in the rain. But that would have taken too long, she reasoned, and she was here. Somewhat cold, wet around the wrists, but here.

Brushing dripping strands of hair from her brow, she filled the pots with water, clamped the flashlight under her arm and began to retrace her steps. One part of her hoped the men would be delayed that little bit longer so that she might have hot soup ready; the other part prayed they'd just *be* there.

She was halfway back to camp and treading cautiously over the wet brush when the sound of something thrashing through the brush brought her to a frozen halt. Eyes wide, she trained her flashlight ahead, then glanced frantically around for a place to escape the big brown bear that surely approached.

The figure that emerged as she stood paralyzed was indeed large and might have been brown, or black—it was hard to tell in a rain-soaked poncho— but, though angry, it was no bear.

"Jordanna! My God, that was a dumb thing to

do!" Patrick growled, stomping the last few feet to her and seizing her shoulders as though he would shake her. "I thought I said we traveled in groups. It's pitch-black and pelting rain and the path's poorly marked—"

"I thought you were a bear!" Jordanna breathed, so relieved to find he was not that she couldn't have cared if Patrick had indeed shaken her. Heedless of his dark mood, she sagged against him. Within seconds his arms slid around her back.

"You scared the hell out of me!" he muttered. The gruffness in his voice gave further credence to his words, even as his arms tightened protectively.

Jordanna buried her face against his throat as it lay exposed through the small V of his poncho. "You saw my note."

"Yeah. Just when I'd finished an ordeal of my own. I knew exactly how wet it was. And how dark. The spring's a good ten minutes from camp. You might have gotten lost!"

"I have a good sense of direction."

"You should have waited till we got back. One of us would have gone for water."

"I wanted to have something warm waiting." She was aware of the musky smell of Patrick's neck, unable to draw away even as her initial fright receded. The strength of his body was compelling. She relaxed against him, stealing precious moments of support as she might a forbidden luxury. "I couldn't sit still. I was worried. What kept you?"

He inched his chin against her hood until her forehead was bared to his jaw. "The rain. We found shelter under a grove of trees and kept hoping it would let up. Then the guys started arguing." A hint of humor entered his voice. "Don wanted to move on. Larry wanted to wait. John tried to reason the whole thing out with the two of them."

"And Bill?"

"Bill was really funny. He kept eyeing the sky, then the ground. You could see him calculating his chances. When the other three had reached an impasse, he growled and set off. We followed."

"Good for Bill."

"Not really. He was so hell-bent on being the leader that he missed a step, stumbled on a tree root and fell headlong into the mud."

"Oh, no!" Jordanna tipped her head back. "Was he hurt?"

Patrick's eyes locked with hers in the dark. "Only his pride. Poor guy. He's real big on physical agility and coordination. It's a good thing you weren't there; he would have been mortified. He felt a little better when I tripped trying to help him up."

"*You* tripped?"

"I do sometimes. I'm not perfect." His message went far beyond a simple slipping in the mud. As Jordanna melted beneath his gaze, he raised a hand to brush her wet cheek. "I'm human. I've got faults. Not the least of which is this insane attraction to you." His voice thickened. "So help me, it's a good thing those guys are around. If not I would have stayed at the shelter making love to you all afternoon."

Jordanna felt the warmth of his breath by her lips and couldn't demur when the hand he left on her back lowered, pressing her intimately closer. "It's a good thing the guys *are* around," she whispered, totally intoxicated by that same insane attraction. "I just might have let you."

"God, Jordanna!" he rasped, using both arms again to crush her against him. "Don't say things like that."

"Why not?" she murmured against his neck. "You say them."

"Yeah. I'm a man. I'm the lusting beast here. Since I can't exactly hide my physical state, I've got a right to speak my mind. But you're a woman. You're supposed to be the sensible one. You're supposed to tell me how crazy it is, how it would never work. You're supposed to push me away from you when I say things like that."

"I can't. I've got buckets of water in my hands."

Patrick held her back to stare disbelievingly at the objects in question. "Damn it!" he exclaimed, coming to life. "Let me take those!"

"It's okay," she reassured him quickly. In truth, she wanted him to hold her again.

But he grabbed the pots and tossed his head toward the path. "You lead the way with the flashlight. I'll be right behind you."

Lest she protest too much and make an utter fool of herself, Jordanna turned and began to pick her way along the hidden path. It took all of her concentration, which was a lucky thing. Otherwise she might have dwelled on her physical attraction to Patrick, and she didn't want to do that. She wanted to relax, to get the most out of her vacation, to fully appreciate her time in the fresh outdoors.

The rain continued at a torrential pace. The path was mucky and dark. It was colder than she would have believed possible without downright snow, and her hiking shoes were not terribly dry when she and Patrick finally arrived at the shelter. Fresh outdoors? She wondered, as she headed directly for her pack and dry clothes.

Any dissension the men might have experienced during their return from Red Brook had been long since forgotten. Having already changed into dry things—leaving their wet ones strung on a make-shift clothesline, which offered Jordanna privacy of sorts—they were gathered around the stove in lively discussion of their admirable fishing skills. Jordanna listened with one indulgent ear, the other waiting to hear Patrick's voice. When it was noticeably absent, she wondered if he too was changing clothes. On the other side of the line? She shot a glance through the legs of a pair of pants but saw nothing. And heard nothing. Between the patter of the rain on the roof overhead and the men's constant chatter, she would have been unable to hear the swish of a shirt leaving his chest, the rustle of denim leaving his legs.

But he wasn't changing. Not yet, at least. Only when his tall form ducked between two sodden shirts did she realize that his pack was on her side of the shelter. Sitting cross-legged on the floor trying to assess the damage to her shoes, she looked up in surprise.

Patrick took one look at her and halted abruptly. "Uh. I'll come back later."

"No. No. It's all right."

"Jordanna...." His voice held taut warning, carrying with it an instant reminder of his words in the woods. Glancing down, she realized that she wore nothing but her long underwear. Though she was suitably covered from neck to ankle, the clinging fabric did nothing to hide any of her curves.

As casually as she could, she swiveled on her seat and reached toward her pack for a dry shirt. "It's all right," she repeated, her voice less sure. Her pulse was suddenly racing, and she knew well its cause. For a minute she heard nothing but the sounds of her own ferreting, a ferreting that seemed to produce nothing but a mess in her pack. The light of the lantern played off the roof to cast her in the palest glow. It was enough for her to see what she was doing. Enough, she knew, for Patrick to see her too.

She had finally managed to find the warm pull-over she'd been seeking when a pair of wet denim legs planted themselves directly before her. Seconds later, Patrick was on his haunches and she raised her eyes.

"You look so damned sexy," he whispered, making no attempt to hide the reluctance of his admission. It should have been a warning. But it wasn't. The reminder that their mutual attraction shouldn't exist did nothing to still the excitement his raking gaze sent through her limbs.

She sat still, afraid to move for fear he'd look away. It was improper. It was unwise. But she wanted him to see her. More, she wanted him to touch her. Her body cried for his touch in a way she had never experienced before.

She was almost relieved when he reached out to stroke her shoulders, then caught her breath when his hands fell to trace the fullness of her breasts, which strained against the constricting fabric, nipples hard and wanting. When his hands moved over her rib cage, she bit her lip in frustration, then held her breath again when he shaped his open palms to the flare of her hips.

Suddenly his touch was withdrawn and he tore at the buttons of his heavy wool shirt. In seconds the shirt was on the ground and his T-shirt over his head and tossed aside. Then he reached for her, bringing her to her knees and flush against him while his hands tugged her shirt up just high enough to allow her breasts to feel his naked warmth.

"Oh, angel," he moaned in a tormented whisper, moving her ever so slowly against his breadth.

Jordanna thought she'd die at the intimate glory of skin on skin. Her limbs trembled wildly. She might have fallen back to the ground had he not held her so firmly. His thumbs found the undersides of her breasts, tipping them higher against him.

"Say something," he urged in an agonized tone.

"I can't. You ... take my breath ...."

"Tell me to go away."

"I can't."

"Scream. Cry rape."

She was breathing in tiny gasps, sliding her hands along the muscled cords of his back in an attempt to know as much of him as possible in the few clandestine moments they had. "You feel ... so good ...."

Suddenly their idyll was interrupted by loud laughter from the other side of the shelter. It was followed by a spate of guffaws interspersed with words enough to assure Jordanna and Patrick that they were, as yet, undiscovered.

Patrick flinched, as though something inside him had snapped. Burying his face in her hair, he groaned. "I'm going to touch you again, Jordanna. Not now. But later." His husky whisper held a shadow of desperation. "I'm going to touch you and kiss you and look at everything I've only been able to lie awake at night imagining. And I'm going to make you want me so badly that you'll never remember there was another man in the world. Then I'm going to make love to you, over and over again, in ways Peter Kirkland never dreamed."

Against the inflammatory effect of his words, mention of Peter's name was chilling. Patrick had intended that. She knew he had. And she wasn't entirely sorry. Something had to bring them to their senses. *What were they doing?* Here, in a rustic shelter, with nothing to separate them from four other men but a line of wet clothes and darkness—here, in a make-believe world, temporarily isolated from a reality in which neither would want the other—*what were they doing?*

"Thank you," she murmured, dismayed and suitably chastised. Belatedly pushing herself from his grasp, she tugged down her shirt and hung her head. Her breasts still throbbed, her body continued to burn where he'd touched her...and where he hadn't. She took an unsteady breath. "I guess I got carried away."

"I guess we both did," Patrick growled, surging to his feet and turning his back on her.

Looking up, she watched the rise of his shoulders, the expansion of his back as he took an extended drag of air. She'd felt his body's need, the tautness that moments before had spoken of his heightened state. She could imagine his frustration. Lord knew her own was great enough.

Averting her gaze once again, she sought her pull-over and slowly drew it on over the thermal jersey. Then, with a diligence born of confusion, she directed her thoughts toward Peter, picturing his arrogant grin, recalling his preening narcissism, his selfish lovemaking. All were things she'd pushed from mind for years, unpleasant things, things she didn't want to remember. Patrick Clayes made her remember.

Patrick Clayes. He'd been Peter's longtime rival. He was a man who'd strived for glory as Peter had done. She shouldn't want him. Shouldn't want any part of him. But she did.

At the sound of a snap, then a zip, her eyes shot up. Patrick had turned back to her and was in the process of wrenching wet denim from his legs. Though his face was shadowed, she felt his gaze. And she couldn't look away.

He said nothing, simply freed himself of the heavy jeans, tossed them onto a bunk, then approached his pack wearing only a pair of dark briefs.

He was the image of uncompromising masculinity, every bit as perfect of form as Jordanna had somehow feared he'd be. Swallowing hard, she reached for dry pants of her own and leaned back to slip them on. Though the men continued to talk on the far side of the line, it was heartstoppingly quiet in the small space she and Patrick shared.

"Pat?" she whispered, hearing the rustle of clothing as he dug into his pack.

"What?"

"I...I'm sorry. I shouldn't have let that go on the way it did."

She waited in a silence broken at last by the rasp of his zipper as he pulled on dry jeans. "I meant what I said," he announced quietly.

When she looked over at him, he was thrusting his arms into the sleeves of a thermal shirt. The snap of his pants lay open; it was all she could do not to focus there. Mouth dry, she pressed her lips together and tried to think of something sensible to say. Nothing came. For a fleeting instant she wondered where the self-confident, worldly-wise woman she'd thought she was had gone. Then time ran out and Patrick was on his haunches again.

"It's too late, Jordanna," he whispered. He didn't touch her. He didn't have to. His brand was intangible, inevitable. "You should have fought me. But you didn't. So I know. I know that you want me. And I'll have you, mark my words. I've been a competitor far too long to turn down a challenge. And when it comes to the prospect of besting Peter Kirkland, no challenge could be sweeter."

Unable to believe the twist of his thoughts, Jordanna was astounded. "I don't believe you said that," she breathed, more hurt than anything. "You'd take me...*to best Peter?*"

His expression unfathomable, Patrick stared at her for a minute, then pushed himself up and stalked away under the clothesline without saying another word.

OF THE CHALLENGES Jordanna had herself faced, none was greater than acting calm and collected through a lively dinner with the guys. Though the trout was delicious, she was able to make no more than a minimal dent in the portion Larry had triumphantly presented her. Rather, she pushed it dutifully around on her plate, hoping none of the men would notice. They did.

"Jordanna's not eating," Don observed. "She doesn't like our trout."

"Maybe she doesn't like fish," John reasoned.

"No," Bill countered. "She just doesn't appreciate the effort that went into this particular meal. She should have been out there with us, freezing her butt off at the edge of a godforsaken river."

"The fish is fine," she insisted.

"Then why aren't you eating?" Larry asked.

"I'm not hungry, I guess. You all did do more work than me today. It's no wonder you're famished. It really is delicious. Honest. I've just had enough." She avoided Patrick's gaze for all she was worth.

Bill grinned. "They had a fight. I told you there was something going on behind the clothesline."

"Bill..." John warned.

But Donald was on the same wavelength as Bill, fascinated by the way Jordanna had involuntarily flinched at Bill's remark. "Really, Jordanna," he said, lips twitching as he leaned close in a brotherly way, "you've got to be careful of guys like Clayes. They've got one thing on the mind. Must have something to do with the locker-room mentality."

They were teasing her, enjoying her discomfort. She shot a glance at Patrick. His smug grin didn't help. Then again, perhaps it did. "You got it," she quipped. "Locker-room mentality. As a matter of fact, I'm surprised you fellows aren't worried yourselves. I hear homosexuality is—"

"Homosexuality?" Patrick yelped.

Larry chuckled. Donald and Bill laughed aloud. Only John looked from Jordanna to Patrick in speculation.

"She got us, didn't she?" Bill mused, then shook his head and laughed again. "I say it again, Clayes. You can have her. She's got an answer for everything, hmm?"

"Almost," Patrick said, his good humor obvious with the gleam in his eye. "Almost."

Only Jordanna—and Pat—knew she'd lost that round.

Long after the coffeepot had been drained, the men continued to sit around the stove reminiscing about past trips, past adventures. Jordanna sat on her bunk with a book in one hand, a flashlight in the other. She tried to get comfortable, but neither the Ensolite pad nor her sleeping bag seemed to provide much of a cushion against the hard wood. She wondered how she'd ever sleep and wished she hadn't napped that afternoon. She was wide awake and alert, though she'd read the same page four times without absorbing a word.

It didn't help that Patrick sat on his bunk not six feet from her, turning page after page of his own book. Nor did it help that each time she dared a glance at him he met her gaze.

There was a purposefulness to him. She felt that quality in the very fiber of her being. And she was all the more confused. When she'd first set eyes on him three days before, she'd instantly associated him with Peter's world, only to find unexpected differences. Patrick was softer, more sensitive, more generous. She'd thought. Until this afternoon.

Strange, she mused, how his words had stirred her at first. She'd never had a man announce his intentions so bluntly, with that hint of fierceness that made it all the more exciting. Lord knew Peter hadn't spared the effort, but then Peter had always gotten what he'd wanted when he'd wanted it.

Turning the page, she stared blindly at the printed words. Oh, yes, Patrick's aggressiveness had excited her... until he'd thrown in that remark about taking sweet revenge on Peter. Something had turned sour in her stomach then. The thought had never occurred to her that Patrick might be using her....

A tiny moan of dismay slipped from her throat. She shifted restlessly on the bunk. She felt Patrick's eyes on her and studiously avoided them, feigning intense interest in the book in her lap. When she could take the pretense no longer, she clapped the book shut, snapped her flashlight off, pushed herself from the bunk and wandered to the front of the shelter.

The rain had eased to a drizzle. The air was raw. Wrapping her arms around her middle, she turned back, gave the men a passing glance and returned to her bunk, where she stretched out in her sleeping bag and prayed for the sweet escape of sleep.

It eluded her. An hour passed. The men one by one went to bed. Patrick had long since turned off his flashlight to lie, much as she did, silent in the night.

Another hour passed. The campsite was quiet. The only raindrops to hit the roof now were those dislodged from branches overhead by the breeze.

One of the men began to snore. Jordanna twisted on her bunk, drawing her sleeping bag to her ears in an attempt to drown out the sound. When the tactic failed, she shifted again.

Then there was a hand on her shoulder and an accompanying whisper. "Jordanna?"

She didn't budge even so much as to free her face from the sleeping bag. "Mmm?"

"The rain's stopped. Want to go for a walk?"

"No," was her muffled reply.

"Why not?"

"After what you said before, how can you even ask that?" She gave a harsh laugh. "You'd drag me to the nearest rock and ravish me. And you'd be right. Peter never did that. He wouldn't dream of taking a week off and going into the woods with me. No press."

"That's what I want to talk about."

She remained silent for a minute. When he didn't continue, her curiosity bested her. "What?"

"Peter. And you."

"No."

Again there was a silence. When Patrick spoke again, his voice held that vulnerability she couldn't ignore. "We've got to, Jordanna. Too much is happening. You need to talk...and I need to hear what you have to say. Come on. We'll just talk. I promise I won't lay a finger on you."

She wanted to say no, then realized how childish it would sound. After all, she couldn't sleep. Evidently, neither could Patrick. And he was right. She'd come to understand the depth of his feelings because of what he'd told her of his past. Perhaps if she explained about her past, Patrick would understand her better.

Very slowly she lowered the sleeping bag from her face. "Just talk?"

"I promise. Please?"

In the end, she agreed only in part because of the exquisitely gentle nature of his plea. The greater part reflected her own need to share that aspect of her with him. Extricating herself from her cocoon, she reached for her jacket, pulled on her shoes, wool hat and mittens and let Patrick lead the way from the shelter.

The woods were quiet after the storm, its evidence the gleaming of wet branches in the moonlight and the soft squish of the ground underfoot. At a low boulder some distance from the campsite, Patrick spread out his poncho and gestured for her to sit. When she'd done so, he joined her, leaving ample room between them as proof of his promise.

"Tell me about it, Jordanna," he said then. "About you."

She shrugged. "Where do I begin?"

"With Peter."

Nodding, she looked off into the distance. Her mind followed suit. "I was nineteen, just finishing my freshman year in college. I was at a party. He made an appearance with someone else. Naturally, we were all enthralled. He was a national hero, a football star in the big time. I was as curious as the rest. He was a celebrity. And very good-looking."

"How did the two of you get together?"

She frowned. "I'm not really sure. I mean, I was enamored of him from the start. What he saw in me, I wasn't so sure. I was a nobody—oh, attractive enough, I guess, but I'd come from nothing and was at college on scholarship simply hoping to get my degree and some kind of a stable job."

"You wanted a career."

"What I really wanted was a husband. And kids. But having grown up in a household where both my parents worked out of necessity, I assumed I'd be doing the same. I wanted that kind of security." She paused for a minute, trying to express herself as honestly as possible. "I'd be lying if I didn't say I had dreams of marrying a wealthy prince. You know— the Cinderella syndrome."

"But you didn't have a stepmother and three ugly stepsisters."

"No. My mother was—is—lovely. And I was an

only child. But young girls have dreams." She paused. "Anyway, by the time I'd entered college I'd pretty much gotten over them. Then Peter came along."

"That party."

"That party. For whatever his reasons, he singled me out. Later he told me that it had been my, uh, my innocence that had appealed to him. I was quieter, more shy than most of the women he'd known." She hesitated. "I was a challenge, he said." She emphasized the word, knowing she'd scored a point against Patrick when he winced. "He asked me out. We became an 'item,' so to speak."

"How did you feel about that?"

"Oh, it was mind-boggling, all right. 'Renowned football hero falls for small-town college girl.' The understatement. It was more like a sack. I didn't have a chance. He knew all the right things to do and say. He had me perfectly psyched. It was seduction in its most perfect form, and I fell for it hook, line and sinker."

"But he did love you."

"Uh-huh." Her voice softened. "He did. That was the one thing I always knew. That was where my true innocence came into play."

"What do you mean?"

"Knowing that Peter loved me, knowing that I loved him, I was totally vulnerable. Carrying on a long-distance affair was devastating. When he asked me to marry him, I was thrilled. He wanted me to be his wife, to be with him always. Giving up school seemed like nothing compared with the prospect of being full-time with Peter." She stopped then, recalling those early days of happiness.

"What happened, Jordanna?"

"Oh, it was wonderful at first. A storybook wedding, complete with a long white train, hundreds of guests, flowers and photographers galore. My parents were proud as punch that their daughter had married a man who could take care of her in the style they'd always dreamed about."

"And you?"

"I was proud too. I was Mrs. Peter Kirkland. I went everywhere with the man I adored. People recognized me, respected me. It was everything I could have hoped for."

Patrick read her pause well. "Except...?"

"I was Mrs. Peter Kirkland. That was all."

"And it wasn't enough."

She lowered her head and spoke very softly. "No. It wasn't. I was bored."

"With *Peter*?"

The barest hint of awe in his voice was revealing. With a wave of insight Jordanna realized that though Patrick might have deeply resented Peter for having stolen the limelight time and again, he nonetheless couldn't deny his admiration for the other man's achievements. In other circumstances, she sensed, Patrick would have revered Peter as many another had done. It was a clue as to Patrick's self-image...and the nature of the battle he'd had to fight over the years.

"Perhaps boredom is too strong a word," she explained cautiously. "Frustration is probably more accurate. I grew frustrated with the kind of life we were leading—running all over creation during the off-season from one fund raiser to the next, one party to the next, one publicity gimmick to the next. During the season it was worse. Because, despite what Peter had promised, I *was* alone. I didn't go on the road with him—I was too distracting, he said. But he insisted I be at the airport to meet him when the team returned, that I be in attendance at press conferences and on his arm for the inevitable pictures. I was the epitome of the loving wife whose only purpose on earth was to welcome her husband home with open arms.

"All the while I was wondering what had happened to the man who had once upon a time stolen quiet moments for us. There were very few quiet moments after we were married. Even when we were home alone Peter's mind was on the next game, the next endorsement, the next awards presentation, the next interview. He swore he loved me, but in truth he loved himself. My presence in his life was much like that of his shiny black Ferrari. He loved that too. It was part of his image."

"You sound bitter."

"Wouldn't you be?" she responded, the hurt still in her voice. "Tell me something, Patrick. You say you've sworn off everything to do with football. Why?"

"Because I've outgrown the sport."

"The sport? Or the life-style that goes along with it?"

He thought for a minute, his dark brow creasing. "Both, I guess."

"But why?"

"I hurt my knee."

"Beyond that. You were always one to avoid the media. Why?"

"Because the media twisted things. It created pictures that weren't terribly accurate. It was shallow—"

"Right! That was my life in a nutshell. Shallow. Shopping expeditions to buy a dress to wear one night. Cocktail parties with the same boring people over and over again. A pretty house. A plastic smile for the press." Her voice lost its edge then, growing low, sad. "There were too many times when I'd sit at home alone in that pretty house wearing pretty clothes...and no smile at all. It was an empty existence, Pat. At least for me it was."

"What about a family? Didn't you want children?"

"Very much. Not Peter."

"That's strange. I would have thought two kids, a station wagon and a dog would add to the image."

"That was what I thought. But he said that kids would be too restrictive. That we wouldn't be able to go out as much. That we'd be tied down. I think," she stated slowly, "that he couldn't bear the thought of sharing my attention. And I don't say that out of arrogance. That was the only conclusion I could reach after months and months of soul-searching."

"Was that when you decided to divorce him?"

"Oh, no. I didn't consider it just grounds for divorce. I rationalized that there had to be another solution to my dilemma."

"Which was?"

"Work." She snorted. "Peter didn't agree. He was against the idea from the start. I'm sure that jealousy was a factor there too. A child. A job. Same difference. Peter simply said that *his* wife didn't work. Wouldn't be good for the image."

Patrick pondered her words before directing the next. "Then what *did* bring about the divorce?"

His gentle voice had a calming effect, the same effect, Jordanna realized, that it had had on her from the start of her dissertation. She'd never talked with another person about her marriage as she did now, yet the words flowed freely.

"It was everything. Snowballing. Things came to a head at a party one night. The team was there, along with the usual hangers-on. I overheard two guys talking about Peter and me. How devoted I was. Remarkable, they said, given Peter's, uh, other interests."

"Other women?"

Jordanna shivered. When Patrick opened his coat in an offer of warmth, she wavered.

"I won't do anything," he assured her softly. "Just help you warm up."

At that moment, Jordanna needed his comfort as well as his warmth. Slowly she slid sideways to rest against him.

"I wondered if it was drugs, at first," she went on meekly. "Or alcohol. Or even some kind of sexual perversion. Anything...but another woman."

"Was there one?"

"Not one. Many. One-night stands across the country. Oh, he was careful. Nothing ever made the papers. He swore it was all meaningless, that I was the one he loved."

"He *told* you about it?"

"Sure. He was arrogant enough to think it wouldn't matter. That was when I realized he'd bought it all. He saw himself as the king. And the king could do no wrong." Her chin dropped. When Patrick pressed her head to his chest she didn't protest. "It hurt, Pat. You can't imagine how it hurt."

"I know, angel," he crooned softly. His arm tightened on her shoulder. "I know."

"I tried after that, but it didn't work. My self-image was crushed. I'd had the illusion that our love was all that mattered. But suddenly I couldn't bear sitting in the stands cheering the bastard on. I had no patience for his parties, even less for his teammates who condoned everything he did, probably lived that way themselves. And the nights alone, well, they were nightmares. I was sure that the world knew everything and was laughing at me. It was paranoid, I know, but I couldn't help it. Even Peter's declaration of love didn't help. I came to the realization that we defined the word in very different ways. I also came to the realization that I was on the verge of a nervous breakdown. *That* was when I moved out. It was a move of self-preservation, the survival instinct at work."

"You certainly did survive," Patrick murmured, squeezing her shoulder in encouragement. "Look at what you've done."

With a shake of her head, she released her hold on the past. "I do have that. Willow Enterprises has given me my life. I don't know what I would have done without it."

"You might have met a nice, ordinary man and fallen in love again."

"No. Not again. I'm not sure I could trust love the second time around."

"Then you've given up the idea of having a family?"

"The business is my family. I've got wonderful people working with me, and each time we launch another product it's like giving birth to a child."

"Not as warm. Not as loving. Or lasting."

"We can't have it all," she whispered sadly, then caught herself. "The business is a constant challenge. It doesn't give me time to dwell on what might have been."

"And in the future? What then? What happens when you're older and more tired and want to settle back and enjoy life with the resources you've earned for yourself?"

"I'll do it."

"Alone?"

"If that's how it turns out. As long as I have my self-respect, I can live with myself." She wanted to sound positive but somehow the words didn't come out that way. As her thoughts tripped into the future, she felt a strange hollowness. Unconsciously, she nestled closer to Patrick.

"Come on. Let's go back to camp. You must be tired."

Strangely, she was. Having poured out so much, she felt drained. Relieved, but drained.

With a nod, she let Patrick help her up and said nothing when his arm remained around her for the walk back through the woods. They reached the shelter to find the men all sleeping. A soft snoring persisted.

"God, I wish he'd shut up," Jordanna murmured under her breath.

"Don't know which one it is or I'd give him a shove."

"How are we going to sleep?"

"I've got one way." Without further word, he worked in the dark to draw the two empty sleeping bags onto the floor and fasten them together. Jordanna watched, knowing what he was doing, reluctant to object if for no other reason than for fear of shattering the warm bond that momentarily existed between them. He'd listened to her story with compassion; that had meant a lot to her. He had to see things from the other side, yet he hadn't sat in judgment. He hadn't proclaimed her the ungrateful bitch Peter had. She felt unbelievably close to Patrick at that moment.

Removing her outer clothes without the slightest hesitation, she slid into the haven Patrick offered. She knew he wouldn't try to make love to her. She knew he was no more in the mood for it than she was. Rather, as she snuggled contentedly against his strong frame, she sensed that he needed her warmth just as she needed his. It was a very private, very personal, very mutual giving. There was nothing one-sided about it.

She didn't hear the snoring from the other side of the shelter. She didn't hear the lonely cry of the wind. All she heard was the steady beat of Patrick's heart. Then, wrapped tightly in his arms, she fell asleep.

5

WHEN JORDANNA AWAKENED the next morning, she was alone with the memory of Patrick's warm body sheltering her through the night. He was long gone, already dressed and at work on breakfast. The other men were just rising.

Her cheeks flushed lightly at the thought of what might have happened had she and Patrick been caught nestled together in their sleeping bag for two. Even now she could hear the razzing. They'd never have heard the end of it.

But they hadn't been caught. Patrick had made sure of that. As the men one by one tugged their clothes from the line, she stole a glance toward the stove. He was on his haunches, immersed in his work. His faded jeans hugged his legs; his plaid wool jacket celebrated the sinewed strength beneath. With his dark hair licking his collar and his large hands deftly manipulating the pot, he looked like a logger, a trapper, a mountain man at ease with himself and the world.

She was envious. And stirred. That the simple sight of him should arouse her was unfair. But it was fact. Had she not been so tired last night, she might have had quite a time falling asleep. He'd been tired too. But if it hadn't been so? Would he have been ... using her?

Stifling a shiver, she quickly dressed and escaped to the stream to wash. When she returned, breakfast was ready. Momentarily apprehensive at meeting

Patrick's gaze, she took longer than necessary in stowing her gear. But she couldn't stall forever. With a deep breath for courage, she headed toward the stove.

She might have been one of the men. Patrick gave her no more than a passing glance as he handed her a cup of coffee. Just as well, she reasoned, accepting the brew and a man-sized helping of hot cereal, which she proceeded to down. She was hungry, and the day ahead would be rugged hiking all the way, Patrick said.

It proved to be so. The trek was tough, if breathtakingly beautiful. Skirting the bog outlying No-Ketchum Pond, they followed the forest trail for a stretch before descending into Perkins Notch. From there they began to climb on a leaf-strewn path, encountering more evergreens as the air thinned. After another descent, they rose again, this time toward Carter Dome, whose summit offered a view of the Wildcat Range and, beyond, the majesty of Mount Washington. It was here that they paused for lunch.

The sun shone brightly. Despite the altitude, the air was surprisingly warm. "Typical New England weather," Patrick explained in rationalizing the contrast from yesterday's storm.

Jordanna was warm in more ways than one. With the morning's hike behind them and a rest period in the works, her mind was free to wander. And wander it did. Though she avoided Patrick's gaze, he was there before her in remembered flashes. A hand on her cheek. Lips teasing her nipple through her thermal shirt. The heat of his hair-roughened chest against her breasts.

"That's it!" Larry cried. "Perfect!"

Stunned out of her reverie, she only belatedly became aware that he'd been taking pictures of her. Her cheeks burned. Scowling, she held a hand up to ward him off. "God, Larry! That's disgusting! Creeping up on a person that way!"

"I didn't creep up. I've been walking around taking pictures of everyone for the past ten minutes. You were preoccupied. You and Pat. You should have seen *his* expression."

Her lips thinned. "Before, or after?"

"Both. Brooding before. Furious after...like you." With a grin, he raised the camera again. "Hey, that's great." And snapped, then lowered the black devil. "You're a woman of many faces, Jordanna. Glowing one minute, glowering the next. I should have thought of this sooner." He lifted the camera once more.

This time, Jordanna bolted up and around, right into Patrick. Hands on her shoulders, he steadied her. "Easy, angel," he whispered. "He's just teasing."

"I don't like having my picture taken," she gritted.

"Neither do I, but if you resist, he's apt to want to do it all the more. You're so cool and unflappable most of the time. I think the men would love to see you unsettled."

"Hey, smile, you guys!" Larry called from the side.

Patrick squeezed Jordanna's elbow. In unison, they turned their heads toward the camera's eye. And smiled.

The instant she heard the click, Jordanna's smile vanished. "Was that settled enough?" she murmured for Patrick's ears alone.

"It'll do. See, he's lost interest."

Sure enough, Larry had turned back to the others, all of whom had followed the impromptu photo session, Jordanna now realized, with gusto. Moaning softly, she sat down on the ground again. She was aware of Patrick watching her, wavering, finally returning to his own lunch some distance away, and she wondered why he'd come over in the first place. But of course he'd come to save her from making a fool of herself. Chivalrous.

And why had she been about to make a fool of herself? Because, she realized, Larry had interrupted a pretty heavy daydream. She'd been annoyed and embarrassed. She'd felt utterly exposed. Dangerous man, this white knight of hers. Spawning dangerous thoughts. Very dangerous.

Spearing the single sardine left in her tin, she swallowed it whole.

THE AFTERNOON'S HIKE was as rugged as the morning's had been. Jordanna pushed herself to her limit, ridding herself of unwanted nervous energy. They scaled Mount Hight, then began the torturous climb downward. Her calves ached; her thighs pulsed. Beneath the weight of her pack, her shoulders clamored for relief.

And she began to wonder just why she was submitting to such torture. She'd been a fool to come. One look at Patrick Monday morning and she should have turned and headed straight back to New York. No, on second thought, she should have found the nearest inn and hibernated for the week. She'd needed the rest, the break from routine. But *this*?

Jordanna wasn't the only one to feel the strain. Rest breaks seemed to come more frequently now, prompted for the most part by the men's cries. Once or twice she sensed that Patrick called a halt for her benefit, but if that was the case he made no point of it. Rather, at times, he seemed more like a harsh taskmaster, driving his team on, ever on. She clung to this image. It was a far safer one than that of the eminently virile outdoorsman. Which he was, decidedly. Maddeningly.

The scenery was some diversion. They hiked through forests that had miraculously escaped the logger's ax. Spruce grew tall. Mossy carpets bordered the path. The sun painted dappled patterns on the woodland floor, skittering through graceful birch limbs.

It was late afternoon when they reached Spruce Brook, where they'd be camping for the night. Grateful as she'd never been, Jordanna dropped her pack, then sank to the ground herself. The men had done the same, she noted with some relief.

With a will of their own, her eyes sought Patrick. He, too, was lowering his pack, his back to her. She started to look away, but was held by something in the way he moved. Oh, yes, he seemed as tall and strong as ever. But something marred the fluidity of his movement. She stared, puzzled when he bent to ease the pack to the ground. There was something about the way he straightened, about the way he flexed his back. When he raised a hand to his shoulder, she understood.

An instinct to comfort made her start to rise but she caught herself when he suddenly turned, collided with her gaze and froze. Hand still on his shoulder, he stared hard at her. His message was clear: I'm fine; it's nothing; forget you saw this. Then slowly he lowered his hand, turned away and knelt to open his pack.

Jordanna had no choice but to settle back on the ground again. She wondered how long his shoulder had been bothering him and sensed that his driving them on had been as much for his own benefit as for that of the group he led. Football heroes did that. Injured or not, they played. Pain was part and parcel of the game.

With a quiet snort of disgust, she lay back against her pack, knees bent, and concentrated on healing herself. If Patrick Clayes wanted to martyr himself, let him, she reasoned. Strange, but he hadn't allowed any of them that luxury through the week.

The week. With a jolt of awareness, she realized that the week was nearly done. It was Thursday. Tonight would be their last night in the wilds. Tomorrow they'd complete the circle and head for home. She wondered where the days had gone and felt a twinge of guilt at the begrudging thoughts she'd harbored earlier. Aches and all, it had been a good week. As exhausted as she was now, it was a healthy exhaustion. She hadn't felt as untethered in years.

Turning her head against its makeshift pillow, she peered through her lashes at Patrick Clayes. She wouldn't see him...after tomorrow. That was for the best, she knew, yet she couldn't help but feel the tiniest bit sorry. He excited her. His presence had added something very special to the trip. Pleasure. Anticipation. The same things she felt on entering the office each morning, yet different. Ve-ry different.

"You're looking sad. No. Melancholy."

She twisted her head to find John squatting beside her. Trying not to blush, she managed a crooked smile. "I'm just tired."

"That wasn't exhaustion I saw," he chided, arching a brow. His gaze shifted to Patrick, then returned. He kept his voice low. "You like him. don't you."

It wasn't a question. Jordanna cautioned herself not to overreact. "Of course. Don't you?"

"Not in the same way. I like him because he's personable and intelligent, because he's a good leader. You, well, you see things I don't. I'm a man. You're a woman."

"You've got a point there," she murmured, closing

her eyes in a gesture of nonchalance that didn't fool John for a minute.

"I hope we haven't embarrassed you. Kidding you and all."

"No problem."

"Will you see him?"

"Who?"

"Pat."

Her eyes opened. "When?"

"After this is over."

"Why ever would I do that?"

"Because you look good together."

She gave a dry laugh and told herself to stay calm. "There's a lot more to a relationship than looking good together."

"You've got a lot in common."

"Oh?" she said noncommittally.

"Football and all."

"I don't have anything to do with football."

"You did."

"Yeah. And I don't want any part of it now."

"Neither does he." John's gaze darted across the campsite to Patrick, who was mixing Tang. "He stuck to his guns. I have to hand it to him. He said he wouldn't talk shop and he didn't." He looked back at Jordanna. "Did he with you?"

"Nope."

"Because you didn't want him to."

"Right."

"And you don't find him attractive?"

"Hey, what is this?" Jordanna asked softly. "An inquisition?" If the questions had come from one of the other men, she might have been offended. Somehow it was different with John. He was the most thoughtful of the group. She was actually curious about what he had to say.

"Of course not. I was just wondering. It's kinda

nice, when you think of the possibilities. If you and Pat were to get together—"

"We're not getting together," she interrupted. "Our lives are too different."

"How do you know that?"

"I know."

"I think you're building a wall that may not exist."

Jordanna spoke softly, without malice. "I think you're overstepping your bounds."

"You may be right. But I like you, Jordanna. You're a very strong, together woman. I admire the way you've put up with us all week. And I can understand what Craig's been raving about. You're intelligent. And determined. I can see why Willow Enterprises is a successful concern. I just wonder ...."

When his voice trailed off, she slanted him a glance. "Wonder what?"

"Wonder what outlet you give to the softer side of you."

"Businesswomen aren't soft."

"You are. I've seen it. The way you look at Pat sometimes. Like just now. You saw him rubbing that shoulder. It was all you could do not to go to him."

"You saw that?" she asked, momentarily unaware of what she was admitting.

"I happened to catch that look of alarm on your face. When I followed it to Pat, I understood."

She settled back and closed her eyes. "What you saw was compassion for another human being. I've never claimed to be ruthless."

He chuckled. "I don't think you could be ruthless if you tried. Especially not to Pat."

"Maybe not," was all she said. She kept her eyes closed, worked to keep her pose as casual as possible.

"Well," John continued, "you were right before. I probably have overstepped my bounds. The side of

Pat we've seen this week is only a fraction of the man. When it comes down to brass tacks, he's probably as shallow as—"

"Are you kidding?" Jordanna exclaimed, opening her eyes and half rising in dismay. But her dismay was never greater than when she saw that John was indeed kidding. With a sly grin and a twinkle in his eye, he moved off to give Patrick a hand.

Bill, it seemed, had a bottle of wine in his pack. He'd kept it tenderly wrapped in his clothes for the week and smugly produced it at the start of dinner. Donald, it seemed, had a second bottle similarly squirreled. When the first was gone, he jubilantly uncorked it. Dinner was a merry event indeed.

Merry, Jordanna thought, as in drowning out those melancholy thoughts that John had rightly accused her of harboring. Or rather, trying to drown them out. Somehow it didn't quite work. Yes, the wine warmed and relaxed her, but never quite erased the fact that Patrick was close. It never quite erased the fact that the tent they'd be sharing that night stood apart from the others, waiting. And it never quite erased the fact that though Patrick might be using her she wanted him nonetheless.

She put it off as long as possible. While the men talked, she sat by, eyes alert, fatigue replaced by an overall tingle. When one by one they headed for their tents, she remained. She...and Patrick.

"Tired?" he asked quietly. The small lantern cast shadows over his face, lending a more sculpted look to already rugged features.

"No," she answered as softly.

"Want to talk?" She shook her head. "Take a walk?" She shook her head again. "Play gin?"

"Gin?" It sounded safe enough. "Okay."

Patrick dealt. They played three games. He won all three. Jordanna was still busy pondering the lesson to be had when he stood and took her hand. "Let's take that walk."

"No, Pat—"

"Now." His grasp brooked no resistance.

Loath to fight him, she acquiesced, following him quietly into the night woods until he came to a halt at the crest of a rise. Only then did he drop her hand.

"Wise move," she murmured, scanning the darkness. "You know I can't run. I'd get lost." Though the moon was out, its light was shuttered by the thick growth overhead.

Patrick stood with his back to her and spoke without turning. "You'd find your way. You always do."

He was talking of her life, and she knew it. "I try."

"Could you try tonight?"

Her breath caught for an instant. "Try what?"

Slowly he turned. Though the night hid the force of his expression, his tension beamed her way clearly. "Try pretending that we aren't who we are. That the past doesn't exist. That I never played football and that you were never married to my darkest rival."

"For what purpose?" she heard herself whisper, though the beat of her heart was positively thunderous, making his answer no more than a formality.

"For us, Jordanna. You and me. One night. Together."

She wanted to step back, but her feet were glued to the mossy floor. "Oh, Pat...I don't know...."

"Don't you want it?" There was neither arrogance nor smugness in his voice, but rather a pleading note that made her ache.

"You know I do," she breathed.

"Then why not? For one night?"

"Because I can't. I can't forget."

"Come on, Jordanna. There's no one here. We're miles away from reality."

But she was shaking her head. "I can't forget!"

"It's not that you can't," he stated then, his voice harder. "You won't. You're afraid."

"Damned right, I'm afraid!" she cried, her composure slowly crumbling. "I'm afraid of everything you were, of everything I was. I don't want that again, Patrick. I told you what it was like. I don't think I could bear it!"

Patrick stared at her in a state of confusion, but when he spoke his tone was even. "I'm not offering you anything you've had before. I thought I'd made that clear."

"You also made it clear that you'd be making love to me to get back at Peter."

"I never said that."

"You implied it."

"*You* inferred it, Jordanna. Let's keep this straight. What *I* said was that I'd make love to you like you've never been made love to before—"

"Like *Peter* never made love to me."

"That's right. Like Peter never made love to you. You were married to him and it kills me. It kills me to think of you in his arms. It kills me to think of you in *any* other man's arms but mine. I'm human. I may not be as arrogant as Peter was, but I've got an ego too. And that ego tells me that when I make love to you it's got to be the best thing you've ever felt. I want that. I need that. Don't you see? Any man would!"

"As a challenge, Pat? That was the word you used."

He raked a hand through his hair in frustration. "Of course it's a challenge. Any time a man makes love to a woman it's a challenge. At least it should be. If it's not ... well, what's the use?"

Jordanna was frightened. He had all the right answers. She wanted to believe him, but to do that would have meant dashing the control she'd held over herself for so many years. It would have meant forgetting. And she wasn't sure she could do that.

Sensing the standoff, Patrick gave a low groan, turned and began to stalk back through the woods.

"Where are you going?" she cried.

"Back to camp," he growled without missing a step.

He was about to round a curve and disappear from sight when Jordanna broke into a run. She had no desire to be left alone to the beavers and raccoons and moose and bears. She had to trot to keep up, his stride was so long. When they reached the campsite she watched him duck into the tent. Her pulse raced in indecision. She couldn't stay outside forever. It was cold. The tent provided shelter, her sleeping bag warmth. Wringing her hands, she waffled. Then, with a helpless moan, she followed Pat.

Having tossed his jacket aside, he was in the process of shucking his jeans. Silently she knelt on her sleeping bag and, head down, proceeded to do the same. When she wore nothing but her long underwear, she quickly slid into her sleeping bag.

Eyes adjusted to the dark, she stared at the roof of the tent. Beside her, Patrick shifted repeatedly in his efforts to get comfortable. Finally, cursing softly, he sat bolt upright and raised a hand to massage his shoulder.

This time Jordanna couldn't look the other way. Rising, she pushed his hand aside.

"You don't need to—" he grumbled, only to be interrupted.

"Shh. It's all right," she whispered. "Let me help."

His muscles were hard, bunched beneath her fingers. She kneaded them gently, persistently, but in vain.

"Take off your shirt," she ordered softly. "My hands keep slipping."

For a minute he did nothing. His head was low, jaw clenched. When at last he reached to pull the thermal shirt from its lower half, she helped him. Then his flesh was bare, warm to her touch. Palms flat, she worked at his muscles, then used her fingers in an attempt to relax them. But the more she toiled, the more tense he seemed. She slid her hands to his neck and attacked those muscles with the same gentle firmness.

Nothing. Nothing but the exhilaration of the feel of his skin. Nothing but the enchantment of his strength. Nothing but a temptation that was driving her insane. Only when she realized that her own tension had grown to match his did she stop. And moan softly. And drop her forehead to his shoulder.

"Oh, Pat," she cried, tottering on the edge.

Slowly he reached up, took her hands and drew them down over his chest. Sagging forward, she buried her face against his neck. He smelled so very male. He felt so very male. And at the moment she felt female from head to toe.

Then he was turning, taking her in his arms, crushing her to him. And she was in his sleeping bag, flush against his strength, offering her mouth for the wild abandon of his kiss.

There was nothing else. Just as he'd said. The past might never have been, for the ardor they shared. He kissed her with a fierceness echoed by her own seeking tongue. And he touched with a thoroughness she needed, not denying her breasts, or her hips, or her thighs, or that warmer, waiting spot between her legs.

She was barely aware that he'd thrust her long johns down to her knees until he levered himself up to do the same. By then she was trembling, arching, needing him more than she'd ever needed another being. Her pants slid to her ankles when she raised her knees to provide him the frame he sought. Then he was inside her, hot, hard and throbbing, stopping her tiny cries at her mouth with the force of his own lips.

Jordanna had never known such raw pleasure. Patrick's ragged gasps were as intoxicating as the rhythmic plunge of his hips. She met him at each thrust, needing to be absorbed, feeling her essence flow toward him even as she devoured all he offered in return. And it was plenty. Amid the fury of their joining, she felt his restraint in the trembling of his limbs. And she knew that he awaited her release as a prerequisite of his own.

When it came, it was blinding, a cataclysmic explosion of inner joy made all the greater by his final thrust, by the cry of exaltation he couldn't contain.

For what seemed an eternal bliss, they clung together until, at last, Patrick collapsed against her. His back was slick beneath her palms, his damp chest melded to hers. The soft sounds of their panting filled the small tent, slowing gradually, reluctantly.

Only after a very long time did he slip from her, rolling onto his side, taking her with him.

"I'm sorry, angel," he whispered, burying his face in her hair. She felt the quivering of his arms as he held her tightly. "I'm sorry."

"Sorry?"

"I wanted it to be so good. So long. I wanted to make love to every single inch of you."

"But you did!"

"I wanted it to be so special."

"It was!" Reaching up, she took his face in her hands. "It was." Her lips brushed his, thumbs replacing them when she drew back. For just a minute she hesitated before whispering God's truth. "Peter never needed me quite that way."

Her words hung in the air until, with a moan, Patrick pressed her head to his chest and hugged her so tightly she had to gasp for breath. "Ahh, angel. I didn't want you to think of him."

"But you do. And I want you to know. What just happened *was* very special to me, Pat. I wanted you so badly."

"And I wanted *you*. You know that, don't you? My desire for you has nothing to do with Peter. It's there. It has been since Monday. I'd have wanted you if you'd been married to the Aga Khan."

"I know," she murmured, slipping her knee over his thigh as she felt him grow against her.

He sucked in a breath. "I want you again."

Her smile lit the dark. "I know."

"Are you pleased?"

"Peter never did," she said in the softest, most vulnerable voice. "Not a second time. I always assumed he was too tired. After a while I realized that he was as self-centered in lovemaking as in everything else. His climax was the be-all and end-all. He owed me nothing further." She traced a small circle over Patrick's breast. "I'm telling you this for a reason, Pat. I'm not one to kiss and tell. But I...it flatters me that you want me again." She rushed the words out, feeling vaguely self-conscious. "Especially after what we just had."

"Because of what we just had," Patrick corrected thickly, kissing her brow. "*Because*, angel. It was so good. So right." He paused. "Jordanna...touch me...."

Heat shimmered through her veins. She looked into his eyes and saw that need again. Never, she knew, would she be impervious to it. Lowering her hand between their bodies, she circled him, stroking timidly at first, then, when he strained in delight, with a courage born of her own reawakening ache.

"So good, angel," he murmured, eyes closed before the pleasure of her touch.

Mindful of her own gnawing inner void, Jordanna led him to her, releasing him only as he slid into her warmth.

"That's it," he whispered. With his hands low on her hips, he guided her body. "Mmm."

Though this time was slower, the rapture was no less intense. Having freed a foot from her long johns, she curved it behind his knee. "Yes, Pat... oh, yes...." Each flex of his hips drove her higher.

"You're... uhh... you're gonna be black and blue," he panted. "Damned ground... ahh, angel...."

"More... there... oh, God, Pat, it feels... so good...."

"And this?" Freeing a hand, he found her breast and rolled its turgid peak beneath his thumb.

"Yes!"

"But I still... can't see you..." he managed between thrusts. "What I'd really like... is to spread you out... in the moonlight." Jordanna's soft whimpering gave him but a moment's pause. "Naked on a soft white sheet... and I'd look at you... and love you...."

She threw her arms around his neck and clung to him. Soft cries came in broken gasps from her throat. Her body was on fire, the core of the heat centered at the point of their union. Her every muscle strained for release.

"That's it, angel," he rasped, his own release imminent. "That's it... let it come... oh, yes...." He felt her catch her breath, then expel it brokenly. Seconds later, inspired by her abandon, he did the same.

For a long time after, neither spoke. Locked together in the single sleeping bag, their closeness made up for the end of the divine luxury they'd shared. When Patrick's breathing deepened, Jordanna tipped her head back.

"Pat?" she whispered.

"Hmm?"

"Do you think...?"

"What?"

"Did we...?"

"What?"

Embarrassed, she blurted it out. "Did we make much noise?"

The frown he showered on her was tinged with amusement. "Noise?" Though his voice was low, he made no attempt to whisper as she had. "As in grunts and groans and sighs—"

"Shh! You know what I mean. Do you think... any of the men might have heard?"

He laughed softly. "I doubt it. Listen."

Sure enough, when she trained her ears she caught the sound of a distant buzz saw. Then, puzzled, she listened more carefully. "I don't believe it. *Two* of them snoring tonight?"

"Sounds that way. Even if the other two are awake, they'd never be able to hear a thing over that racket. Not that I care, mind you. It wouldn't bother me if those guys knew."

"It *wouldn't* bother you," she scolded. "You're a man. I can just see you strutting around with your chest puffed out—"

He squeezed her tight to cut her off. "Hey, I didn't say that. I'm not the peacock you'd like to think."

There was an underlying note of annoyance in his voice. Instantly Jordanna resented its cool presence in what was an otherwise warm afterglow of passion.

"I know," she whispered, stroking his chest, unruffling his feathers. "I guess I'm just wary. Must be my early training. I'm sorry."

Rolling to his back, Patrick took her hand in his and pressed it to his heart. "No, I'm sorry. Sorry you had to be trained that way. But we're not all like that. You've got to believe me."

She did, and she told him so. When he seemed to relax, she snuggled closer, twining her legs with his.

"Comfortable?" he asked.

"Mmm. I've got the better part of the deal. You make a good mattress."

"My butt's killing me."

"How about your shoulder?"

"It's better. I guess I forgot about it." He shifted until he was more comfortable all over, then kissed her brow. "Good night, angel."

"Night, Pat."

Closing her eyes, Jordanna drifted off to sleep with an ease that would have astounded her. She should have been thinking of what she'd just done. She should have been pondering the ramifications. She should have been wondering what tomorrow would bring. But she wasn't. She couldn't. The moment was too special to be marred in any way. Tomorrow would come soon enough. It always did.

BRIGHT SUNSHINE and invigoratingly cool air—that was Friday's climatic offering. For some strange reason that wasn't really at all strange to Jordanna when she stopped to think about it the weather did little to cheer her up.

Actually, she'd awoken in good spirits, drifting into consciousness on a cloud of erotic memory. Burrowing closer to Patrick had been her first mistake. When she hit empty space, she opened her eyes. That had been her second mistake.

He was gone, as always. Dressed and out of the tent before the rest of the group had stirred. What bothered her was that she wasn't the rest of the group. She was the woman he'd made love to not once, but twice in the night now past. He might have at least kissed her before he'd left. Then again, maybe he had.

Frowning while she tugged on her clothes, she hit the outside air to find the other men digging into breakfast as though they hadn't eaten in a year. The worst of it, though, was not how or what they ate but rather what they talked about. Going home.

It was Friday. Today they'd be going home.

Jordanna silently neared the group, then stopped. She stood listening, unable to advance, unable to retreat, until Patrick's approach broke her paralysis.

"Freeze-dried omelet?" he offered, holding out a plate.

As the first words he'd spoken to her since his tender "Good night, angel," they weren't the most romantic he might have picked. But it was morning. They had an audience. And Patrick's somber gaze was in keeping with Jordanna's mood.

"Uh...." She looked down, wavering.

He spoke gently. "You'll need something. We've still got a full day ahead."

Without looking up, she accepted the plate, helped herself to coffee and sank down to the ground.

"Shave," Larry was saying as he stroked his grizzled jaw. "That's the first thing I'm going to do."

John shook his head. "Not me. I'm heading for the shower before I touch a thing. I must have half the dirt in New Hampshire under my collar. And damn it, Bill, don't give me that bit about washing up more. The water around here's been frigid."

Bill held up a hand. "Suit yourself. Personally—" he grinned and closed his eyes to dream "—I'm dying to sink my teeth into a nice, thick, juicy, rare steak."

"A bed," Donald injected. "That's what I want. A nice warm bed with a mattress that won't bite."

"How about you, Jordanna?" Bill asked. "What's your pleasure, now that the end's in sight?"

Jordanna's insides knotted. It was all she could do not to look at Patrick. "Oh, all of the above, I guess."

"You guess?" Donald teased. "Hey, where's the opinionated lady who arrived here on Monday? She never would have guessed. She would have known. Or—" he sent a sly glance toward Patrick "—are you two planning to stay up here and do the route again?"

Jordanna couldn't help but peer at Patrick then. He looked as grim as she felt. It was only with great effort that she forced what she hoped passed as a smile for the benefit of the other men. "I'd like that, but it's a luxury I can't afford. I've got a business waiting back in New York. Come Monday morning my work's cut out for me."

"Ah, the executive woman," Donald returned in echo of the words he'd used on Monday. Then there had been disdain in his tone. Now there was respect. Likewise, his smile was warm.

Jordanna nodded, her own smile more natural. These men weren't so bad, after all. Come to think of it, they'd been pretty good sports. Her gaze touched one then another of them, giving silent thanks for their indulgence. When, uncharacteristically self-conscious, she looked down, she knew that something *was* different in her now. Was it the soft side John had mentioned yesterday on the trail? *Had* she been burying it all these years?

She had much to think about as they dismantled the tents, loaded their packs and started out on the trail. It was a relaxing hike. Though the scenery lacked the spectacular quality they'd been privy to earlier in the week, it was pleasant. Emptied of food, their packs were lighter. Hardened by trial, their muscles were silent.

Following the Wild River Trail, they stopped for lunch at a peaceful spot overlooking a clear blue pool that would have been a bather's dream had the day been warmer. Jordanna sat quietly munching on the last of her sunflower seeds, wondering where the week had gone, wishing it had been longer. Oh, yes, she craved a bath. And a bed. And a fresh, warm, buttery croissant. But there were other cravings now, ones she hadn't wanted but ones she couldn't deny.

Patrick said little. She would have given any number of pennies for his thoughts, but they were hidden behind a mask of self-control. As always, he was the consummate guide, directing their sights here and there, talking in that exquisitely patient, ever amiable tone of his.

At times she wanted to scream. _What did you feel? What do you think? Where do we go from here?_ But she didn't. She knew the answers, at least those that applied to her. She and Patrick would go their separate ways. It was understood. It had to be. Here in the wilderness they might be two creatures without restraint. Back in the city, reality awaited.

And reality drew closer with each step they took. Though the afternoon's walk was undemanding, Jordanna felt a rising anguish. She tried to push it aside, to put the week in perspective, to shift her thoughts forward and muster enthusiasm for her return to work. Somehow that didn't work. Just when she thought she'd mastered her senses, she'd catch sight of Patrick and her insides would twist anew.

Too soon they arrived at the campground from which they'd set out four days before. The men were jubilant, as enthusiastic about the trip as they were about taking off their backpacks a final time. There were heartfelt thanks to Patrick, handshakes all around, even hugs for Jordanna, which she returned with sincerity.

Then Donald and Bill took off in one car, Larry and John in another. And she and Patrick were alone.

Car keys in hand, she slowly approached the Jeep as he slammed its tailgate shut and turned. "Got the tents and all?" she asked.

"Yup."

She nodded, looking out toward the woods. "Well, I guess I'd better be on my way."

"Are you driving all the way back tonight?"

"I was hoping to." Hands thrust in her pockets, she eyed the sky. "I'm not sure. What with all that talk about beds and baths, I might just give in and stop at a motel along the way."

There was silence then. Billowy clouds moved in ever changing formation across the sky. Though they were the object of her scrutiny, she saw nothing of their beauty.

"Jordanna?"

Heart pounding, she met his gaze. "Yes?"

"I know of a nice place. It's about an hour away. I thought I'd spend the night there." He seemed to hesitate. "I'm sure they've got plenty of room. Off-season and all...."

She nodded but didn't speak. Her throat was suspiciously tight.

"Well...I just wanted to mention it...." He turned toward his door, then paused, head down, shoulders tense. When he looked back, his eyes spoke of the same inner pain she'd been feeling all day. Reaching out, he cupped her jaw, caressing her cheek with his thumb. "You'd better get going. I'll follow. I'll feel better knowing you've hit the main road okay."

Tipping her head to the side, Jordanna rubbed her cheek against his palm. "No," she said softly. "You go. I'll follow."

She thought she saw a flare of light in his eyes, but it was gone so quickly she wondered if she'd imagined it. She couldn't have imagined his warmth, however. It was a living thing, searching her depths, seeking and finding her heat.

It was that heat that kept her foot on the gas, her eye on the Jeep ahead of her through the hour's drive to the inn he had in mind.

6

WILDWOOD WAS A GRAND OLD INN in southern New Hampshire, set at the far end of its own private road beneath towering elms whose leaves had fallen and majestic firs whose needles had not. Wondering if she'd made the right choice, knowing she truly had no choice at all, Jordanna pulled her rented Chevy to a halt beside Patrick's Jeep in the gravel lot.

He was there to help her out, his expression one of tense anticipation, even uncertainty, if her interpretation was correct. "Let's bring the packs," he suggested quietly. "They'll wash whatever we want." Taking her keys from her, he removed the backpack from her trunk, slung it over one shoulder, secured his own on the other and started up the flagstone path toward the inn's broad front steps.

Jordanna would have protested his carrying both packs, but she caught herself. Divested of sleeping bags and pads, not to mention the food and other equipment that they'd been hauling around all week, the packs weren't heavy. And he was already halfway there, climbing the steps, holding the bright white door open for her.

Trotting to catch up, she preceded him into the stately front hall, then stood aside as he approached the registration desk. He didn't look back, didn't ask if she wanted her own room. It would have been a foolish question. After last night, there could be no pretense between them. This elegant old inn with its high ceilings, turn-of-the-century moldings and graceful winding staircase was a reprieve. Jordanna could no more have resisted it than she could have the vulnerable look Patrick sent her when a bellboy materialized to lead them to their room. She answered it with a tremulous smile, quickly averting her gaze and concentrating on following the bellhop.

Their room was large, dominated by ceiling-high windows and a roomy four-poster bed. A heavily sheened mahogany dresser stood against one wall, a similarly finished desk against another. Before the window was a cushiony armchair upholstered in a large floral print of green, burgundy and white; nearby stood a matching lounge chair. The overall effect was of bright airiness and down-home New England charm. Jordanna knew Patrick had stayed there before. He'd chosen well the site for a tryst.

With their packs deposited on a long luggage rack and the bellhop gone, they were somewhat ill-at-ease. Jordanna's eye skimmed the room again, coming to rest on the bathroom door. Though the late-afternoon sun poured into the room, the bellhop had switched on that light in his brief tour.

She dropped her gaze, focused on her muddy hiking shoes, took in the dirty sheen of her pants, then her jacket. Whether it was the utter cleanness of the room or the simple cumulative effect of five days with makeshift bathing, or the fact that Patrick would be seeing her, truly *seeing* her for the first time, she suddenly felt overwhelmingly grubby.

When she looked up, he was craning his neck against the collar of his T-shirt, using a finger to separate it from his skin.

"I think John was right," she murmured awkwardly. "I feel like I've got half the state's dirt under my clothes."

"Me too," he answered. With deft fingers he reached for the buttons of his wool shirt, releasing one after the other until the shirt hit the floor as the first of the must-wash pile.

With a nonchalance she was far from feeling, Jordanna began to undress in turn. "They'll really wash all this stuff?" she asked, wondering, as she added her once bright lime-hued jacket to the pile, who in his right mind would want to touch it.

"They always have. I've stayed here several times before."

Nodding, she knelt and concentrated on unlacing her shoes. "These were pretty good. I haven't got a blister."

Patrick's T-shirt hit the pile, then he was bending over to remove his own dirt-encrusted boots. "Ah, but were they warm?"

"Pretty much so."

"And dry?"

She set one aside and went to work on its mate. "Except for the day it rained."

He chuckled but said nothing. Standing, Jordanna reached for the Velcro fastening of her pants, hesitated, then tugged it apart. The sound was deafening to her senses. For a split second she wondered if she'd caught some kind of madness that had been floating around in the woods that week. What she was doing was crazy. It was truly *dumb*. But she couldn't stop her fingers when they grasped the hem of her sweater and pulled it over her head. Nor did she hesitate when Patrick's second boot hit the oak floor with a thud.

Eyes still downcast, she slipped the pants from her legs. They no sooner landed atop the pile when they were covered by Patrick's jeans. Pulse racing against a wave of self-consciousness, she shimmied her long underwear down, dropped the warm cloth and, before she lost her courage, dragged the thermal shirt over her head.

It was then that her gaze met Patrick's. He stood before her wearing nothing but his briefs. His chest was broad, lightly tanned, matted by the dark curling hair she'd only felt before. His torso was lean, tapering to his hips. Well-muscled thighs held him straight, while her own trembled mercilessly. Mouth dry, she watched as his gaze fell.

"Do you never wear a bra?" he asked in a husky whisper. His eyes focused with unhidden appreciation on her full breasts.

She raised her hands to her waist, started to wrap them around herself, sheepishly dropped them. "I... I always do. Working, I mean. But on the weekend when I'm alone.... And I thought it'd be an added restraint while I was hiking...."

"It's okay," Patrick murmured, entranced as he took a step forward. His fingers found the hollow of her throat and traced the lightest of lines southward through the valley between her breasts, then up around one swelling mound. "You're beautiful, Jordanna. Have I told you that?"

Her cheeks were pink and warm. "I think you said something of the sort at one point."

"Well, I say it again. And this time I know what I'm talking about." His gaze fell to the line where her panties began. He looked up once quickly, then, as though unable to help himself, looked down again.

Her pulse racing, Jordanna watched his fingertips slip beneath the thin elastic band. With unbelievable grace, he sank to his knees, drawing the silken fabric down until, with a hand on his shoulder for the support she badly needed, she stepped free.

"So beautiful," he murmured again. Sitting back on his haunches, he stared at her. His large hands framed her hips, then slipped behind to gently caress her bottom.

Jordanna's fingers sank into the hard flesh of his shoulders. "I want to be clean for you," she whispered. "I want to be fresh and—"

"You couldn't be more beautiful than you are now. God, Jordanna!" Coming up on his knees, he wrapped his arms around her back and pressed his face into her stomach. "I want you so much I don't think I can stand it."

"You're not standing," she managed in a tremulous whisper. "I'm the one who's standing and I don't think I can much longer." Her knees trembled wildly in rhythm with every one of her nerve ends.

Patrick breathed deeply of her skin, then kissed her navel and forced himself to rise. Against the straining fabric of his briefs, his desire was obvious. "If we don't hurry, I'm apt to take you here on the floor. But I want you soft and comfortable. We've had enough of the ground for a while. And those sheets are too clean and white to even imagine putting these trail-worn bodies on them."

Taking her hand, he led her to the bathroom. There was no sign of a shower. Rather, an ancient porcelain tub stood on its four clawed feet, as beckoning as anything could have been at that moment. Anything, Jordanna mused, except the hard strength of Patrick's body.

Patience, she told herself, though her trembling persisted. Patience.

Propping one arm on the lip of the tub, Patrick turned on the water, tested it, adjusted the taps to ensure the right temperature, then waited for the tub to fill.

Eyes glued to the rising water and hands on his hips, he was more disciplined than Jordanna, who couldn't help but study his body in the bright light. His back was smoother than his hair-spattered chest, his muscles that much more boldly presented. There

was the scar that rounded his shoulder, and a small
birthmark to the left of his backbone. Helpless, she
touched it, then trailed her fingers down the hollow
in the center of his back.

If she'd thought him momentarily preoccupied
with the bath, she'd miscalculated. Turning, he
grabbed her, flattened her against him and began to
tickle. "You want it on the floor? Do ya? Hmm?"

"No...don't, Pat...I give! I give!" The words
were forced out between laughs. When she tried to
evade the devastation of his fingers, he set her back.
The humor that had carried his voice moments before was gone.

"Do you, Jordanna?" he asked softly.

Stepping forward again, unwilling to forfeit one
instant of his warmth, she threaded her fingers into
his hair. "Yes," she whispered. "For tonight, anything...."

Their lips met in a kiss that began gently but esca-
lated until finally Patrick wrenched his mouth away
and bent quickly to the tub. "They might not be
thrilled if this tub overflowed," he grunted, turning
off the taps. "Crawling laundry's one thing. A
flood's something else." Straightening, he turned to
Jordanna. Eyes holding hers, he lowered his briefs
and kicked them off.

Jordanna knew that her breathlessness was not
from the tickling he'd given her moments before.
Swallowing hard, she let her gaze fall. If what she'd
felt, if what had given her such pleasure the night
before had been magnificent, the virile display before her was no less.

"Oh, Pat," she whispered with what little breath
she could find, "you're beautiful too." Inching closer, she put a hand on his chest, then slowly lowered
it until what she'd seen was at her command. The
dignity with which Patrick had endured her scru-

tiny began to disintegrate with his flagrant response to her touch. His arms gently circled her back, muscles quivering in restraint.

"You won't think so in another minute," he growled. "This tile floor's even harder than the wood one out there."

Eyes closed, Jordanna turned in to his chest, kissing him slowly, savoring his textured skin beneath her lips. When her tongue darted out to taste his hard nipple, he jerked.

Taking her face in both of his hands, he forced it up. "The bath?" he suggested.

"Hmm?" She was in a daze of pleasure that had blotted out even the gritty feel of her own body.

"The bath, Jordanna," he repeated, more gently this time as he kissed first one eye, then the other. "I want to be clean for you too, angel. Clean and fresh and smelling of something other than a creature of the wild."

"Creatures of the wild are intoxicating," she said.

"They can be pretty rank."

Her eyes opened. "Were you worried? Last night, I mean?"

"Not then. Well, maybe a little. But when you're out there and you get used to feeling, uh, earthy, things take on their own perspective. Here in this place, it's another ball game."

She smiled. "I do believe you're blushing."

To compensate, he manufactured a scowl. "Would you like a bath, or am I going to take it by myself?"

"I want one. I want one." Turning, she dunked a toe, then a whole foot. "Ahh, hot water." Then she was stepping into the tub and sinking down, moaning at the only other pleasure that might have had a chance against Patrick's masculine allure. "This is heaven!"

"How quickly she changes gear," he teased, staking claim on the opposite end of the tub by folding his large body therein.

Much as he might have been ribbing her, he changed gear with alacrity himself. There was nothing seductive about the way they scrubbed themselves, bandying the soap back and forth as though it was the only thing that mattered. When the water was sufficiently dirty, they stood while it drained. Meeting the physical challenge, they bent to the tap, twisting and contorting, laughing in turn, until both scalps were squeaky clean. Then, rationalizing that they had a right to one bath each, they filled the tub again. This time Patrick stretched out and settled Jordanna between his legs. Her head fell back on his shoulder. His arms lightly circled her stomach. For the moment sexual needs were forgotten.

"Nice?" he murmured against her ear.

"Oh, yes," she replied. Clean and warm, her skin tingled. A delicious languor suffused her limbs. "Peaceful. Very peaceful." It was true. She felt wonderfully at home in Patrick's arms. Closing her eyes, she sighed.

"I agree."

"Peaceful?"

"Your sigh. Relaxed. Lazy. Unable to bear the thought of moving an inch."

And so they lay there, steam from the tub wafting over them. Time passed, but they were oblivious. Eyes closed, nestled together, they prized long moments of pleasure. Only when the water began to cool did Jordanna look down to see tiny goose bumps prickling her breasts.

"I'm thinking the same thing," Patrick mused. "It's about that time."

Setting Jordanna forward, he put a hand on either side of the tub and hoisted himself up, stepped out and reached for the thick terry towels that awaited on the nearby rack. Slinging one over his shoulder, he held the other open for Jordanna.

Suddenly the peace of moments before seemed to evaporate, replaced by the sexual tension they'd encountered before in the bedroom. The bath had been a strange buffer, a thing of necessity. But it was done now. And what was to come?

Jordanna knew. She also knew, with a flash of conviction, that it too was a necessity. She needed another dose of Patrick as badly as she'd needed that bath.

Eyes holding his, she rose from the tub and stepped out onto the mat to be enfolded in the towel he held. He patted her face dry with its ends, his eyes flowing from one to another of her features, worshiping each in turn. When he released the towel to reach for his own, Jordanna continued the work herself. The terry was an abrasive stimulant to her awakening flesh; her pulse quickened with each stroke. As she watched Patrick dry himself, she mirrored his movements. It was as though he, rather than the towel, were touching her. In a sense he was; his gaze followed her actions as hers followed his.

Not a word was spoken, but the air hummed with sensual awareness. In a bid to diffuse its frightening force, Jordanna abruptly raised the towel to her head and, bending from the waist, began to scrub at her hair. Most of the moisture had left it as she'd lain against Patrick in the tub. By the time she was finished with the towel, her short auburn crop was barely damp. Wrapping the towel around her waist, she turned to the mirror and began to finger-comb the thick strands. Within seconds Patrick materialized behind her. His hair was in a like state of semidryness, falling loosely in place, looking daringly rakish.

Catching her raised elbows, he slid his hands down until his fingers touched the side swells of her breasts. Jordanna held her breath and watched in the mirror as he cupped, then gently kneaded them. Her nipples grew taut. Grasping them between thumbs and forefingers, he tugged them until her head fell back and she whimpered in desire. He drew her back then, pressing her snugly against him. His own desire was blatant, his breath came unevenly by her ear. When she would have turned in search of greater satisfaction, though, he stepped back to drop his towel on the sink.

Silently he took her hand and led her into the bedroom where the four-poster bed waited. He tugged back the heavy quilt until the sheets lay invitingly, then turned to her.

Heart pounding so hard she felt he had to be able to see it, she tipped her head up at the guidance of his hands. He seemed about to speak. She held her breath, wondering what words could possibly express the unbridled desire in his gaze. When he simply lowered his head and took her lips, she knew there were none. No words to say how much he wanted her. No words to say she wanted him as much. He knew. They both knew. Given the many doubts they'd left outside, the commitment was there. And potent.

His lips opened hers with ease, tasting the sweetness of her breath, sampling the delicate texture of her mouth. Not for an instant was he still, yet there was nothing frenetic in his kiss. Rather it was a slow, steady exploration of her every nuance, and it made a statement as to his sensual intent. In that moment Jordanna knew that he planned to do everything he'd once said—to touch her, to look at her, to make love to every single inch of her. Even as she feared the depth of the claim she sensed he'd make, it excited her beyond belief.

He raised his head then, lips moist from hers, and spoke again with his eyes in the deep, sultry voice of silence. Jordanna's limbs quivered at his message. When his gaze dropped to the towel that ringed her hips, she bit her lip to keep from crying out. It amazed her that his kiss, his look could do such erotic things, and while she knew she should have expected it by now, she also knew she never would. It was new and different, this heartwrenching attraction to another human being. With Peter, part of the attraction she'd felt had been inspired by the glamour of his position. She saw that now, and for the first time admitted that, despite her disclaimer to Pat, perhaps what she'd seen in Peter had indeed been his particular status in life.

Patrick allowed none of that. He'd made it clear from the start. His appeal was solely in the man that he was—tall, dark, compelling, dignified and reaching for her towel with an attitude of such intense need that she felt she was the only woman on earth who could possibly satisfy him. It was a heady thought. And Jordanna did have ego needs of her own, very special needs that had never quite been met until Patrick had entered her world.

The towel slid soundlessly to the floor and he was lifting her high in his arms, placing her gently on the cool, clean sheets, coming down on one knee by her side. The setting sun spiked golden arrows over her body, pointing to the concave plain of her stomach, the rounded curves of her breasts, the hollow of her throat, which pulsated with each quick breath she took. Warm and firm, his fingers traced each arrow, inspiring sensations within her that spiraled and converged deep down low in her belly. It was all she could do not to reach for him, so great was her mounting heat, but she opened her palms against the sheet instead and, fingers spread, pressed them flat.

Patrick's touch was devastating. His hands covered every inch of her, shaping each curve, exploring each hollow. Then he bent and began to kiss her, starting at her lips before gliding downward. With each sweet inch, the fire within her burned hotter. When she could bear no more of his delicious torture, she grabbed his arms and urged him upward.

He looked at her for a minute then, and she saw what she herself felt. It was the moment. There could be no more waiting. His knees nudged hers apart, he braced himself on his hands. Then, gaze still locked with hers, he thrust forward.

Jordanna's eyes widened, then closed. His brand was hot and firm, searing her insides with a pleasure beyond words or thoughts or dreams. She sighed softly at the satisfaction of it, then met his movements, stroking his powerful body as the heat rose until, at last, fingers clutching his shoulders, she reached the pinnacle of their joining. All the more heady was the knowledge that Patrick was right there with her. He too closed his eyes against the force of the pounding sensation. His great body stiffened, he sucked in his breath, then let it out in short, ragged gasps. Only in time, when the gasps began to lengthen, did he release his hold on himself and sink down onto her slender form. Head buried near hers on the pillow, he lay still as the last aftershocks of his pleasure shook him. Then he turned his face to hers and placed a slightly breathless kiss on her ear.

"That was...."

Jordanna gave a smug, cat-satisfied smile at the way his words trailed off in suggestion that he too was at a loss. "Wasn't it?"

"Umm." Slipping to her side, he left his arm in firm possession of her waist. "You're something."

She felt like something. It was a delightful feeling. "So are you." She layered her arms over his.

They rested that way for a time, the silence offering a peaceful aftermath to the passionate storm of moments before. All that remained of the sun's light was a pale amber glow reminiscent of the lantern in the woods. Rather than hard ground at their backs, though, there was a welcome mattress. And rather than a sleeping bag and tent to keep their secret, there was new freedom. The knowledge that it was temporary did nothing to curb Jordanna's enjoyment of it. She felt warm and sated and very much enthralled by the dark-haired man whose body seemed so right entwined with hers.

"Angel?"

"Mmm?" She smiled at her automatic response to his nickname. It too was new. To Peter she'd been either baby or honey or sweetie or increasingly, as their marriage became strained, just Jordanna.

"Are you sleeping?"

"Uh-huh."

He gave her a playful squeeze. "That's what I thought." With a burst of energy that startled her, he sat up, stretched over her to switch on the lamp, then grabbed the phone.

"What are you doing?" She laughed, loving the solid feel of his body slanting across hers.

He held her off with an upraised finger and spoke into the receiver. "Yes. This is room 206. We'd like to order dinner. A couple of steaks, medium rare, some baked potatoes, salads, whatever fresh vegetables you've got and a quart of milk." He shot a mischievous glance at Jordanna. "The Black Forest cake will be fine. And some coffee. I think that should do it. Twenty minutes. Right." Then he hung up the phone and slowly slid back to his side of the bed.

Jordanna didn't miss the way his body teased hers in retreat. Her feline smile reflected that appreciation. "Sounds like some meal."

He settled her into the crook of his arm. "We deserve it." He drew the sheet up to cover them.

She nestled against his chest. "I am pretty hungry, come to think of it. I don't want to look at anything freeze-dried for a while."

"What's the matter? Not an outdoors girl after all?"

"Now, did I say that? Seems to me you were the first one to think of steak, medium rare."

"Is that okay?" There was a moment's uncertainty in his voice, but she was quick to set him at ease.

"Perfect."

He kissed her brow. "Mmm. So are you."

"Oh, I don't know. I have my moments."

"At work?"

"Sometimes."

"Tell me about it—your work. How did you get started?"

It surprised her that she didn't hesitate. On one level she hadn't wanted to bring the real world into the fantasy she and Patrick lived. But it seemed so right to want to tell him about her life that the words flowed.

"After I left Peter I went into a kind of blue funk. I wasn't sure where to turn. I knew I wanted to do something. I *had* to do something—"

"Wasn't he giving you support money?"

"Oh, yes. Begrudgingly. And I accepted it... begrudgingly. Which was why I was in a rush to find some means of self-support. There was pride involved. *And* a desperate need to do something with my time."

"Did you have Willow Enterprises in mind from the start?"

"Only indirectly. During my time with Peter, I'd met people who suggested that I should start something."

"I can understand it. Classy lady. Influential name. Great visibility. Beautiful to boot."

She raised her head for a minute to scowl. "I didn't see it that way." He returned her head to his chest and left his hand to smooth her hair behind her ear. The gentle intimacy was enough to encourage her to go on. "I looked into lots of things. Had interviews and all. But it seemed I was always at someone else's command. And that was what I'd been trying to escape. So I began to think more and more of starting my own business. When I called the people who'd mentioned it, they were as enthusiastic as ever. Unfortunately, each time I hung up the phone all the negatives crowded back in on me."

"Like what?"

"Like the fact that I'd dropped out of college after my freshman year. Like the fact that I knew nothing about business. Like the fact that starting a business required an investment the likes of which I just didn't have."

"Peter had it."

"Sure he did. And I didn't want a cent. We were getting a divorce, remember?" She took a breath against Patrick's skin and stretched an arm across his waist. His nearness was the reminder she needed that life with Peter Kirkland was indeed behind her. "Anyway, I was hooked. The more I looked for other work, the more I liked the idea of starting something myself. So I began to read. Anything and everything I could find about small businesses. I came to believe that if I could gather the right people around me, they would provide the know-how I lacked. What with my ideas and the contacts I'd made through Peter, we had a fighting chance."

"So you fought."

"Uh-huh. I did. I got a lump-sum settlement from Peter that was enough to start the ball rolling. I rented a small place and hired five women, each of whom had spirit and the right credentials. They became my vice-presidents—sales, marketing, research and so on. We planned everything on paper, then fought dearly for money enough to set the thing up the way we wanted."

"Which was?"

"Solid. And substantial. No cottage industry here. We knew we wanted a class image. From the start we envisioned selling nationwide through the best of the department stores." Pausing, she tipped her head back to meet Patrick's gaze. "Sound arrogant?"

"Not arrogant. Just smart. If you've got the right product and it's marketed the right way, you'd be foolish not to aim high. There's something about a class act that attracts classy people. Basic psychology."

She grinned. "Psychology, baloney! It was common sense. And it worked."

"Sounds like it did. You've done well."

"Well enough to repay the original loans we took. Well enough to go public and expand all the more." Her voice softened in tone but lost none of its pride. "Well enough for me to take out the money Peter gave me and invest it in something in no way connected to the business."

Patrick chuckled. "Good girl. He must've croaked at that."

"I don't know if he even knows, and personally, I don't care. It's what *I* know that counts. It's inside me, Pat. I feel good about myself, about what I've done. I'm a person now, rather than an appendage. It's a very satisfying feeling."

More serious, he studied her urgent expression. "I can see that, angel. I'm happy for you."

She smiled suddenly and pressed her face to his chest to hide her blush. "I get carried away when I talk of the business."

"That's natural. It's your life."

"But I'm usually so busy that I don't think about it this way. It's odd being away from it all and thinking back on it."

"That's what vacations are for. To put things into perspective."

She propped her chin up, humor in her eyes. "Is that so? Funny, I was beginning to wonder if they weren't to pick up strange men and have affairs in the woods."

"We're not in the woods now."

"No."

"Are you sorry?"

"No."

"Good." He captured her lips in a languorous kiss, then, with a growl, pulled her atop him. "I was a fool to think once would be enough. Each time I have you, I want you all the more."

She could feel it, both in her own body and in his. Sliding up over him, she sought his lips again. Her knees fell to the sheets on either side of his thighs. As her tongue filled his mouth, she teased him at that other point where she was so open, so ready. He was addictive; with so little provocation, she needed him again. And as with any addiction, the first and only thing on her mind was to satisfy the craving.

Slipping a hand between their bodies, he found her warmth and stroked her with such knowing care that she had to gasp for air.

"It's not fair, Pat!" she cried, but already he was lowering her hips onto his waiting strength. And then all that mattered was the rhythmic surge of their bodies, the lips that clung, the hands that found each other's sensitive spots and drew everything from them. When with joint cries of release it was over, they lay spent, Jordanna's damp body limp above his, which was no more energized.

It was then that room service knocked.

"I don't believe it," Patrick groaned.

Jordanna laughed breathlessly. "I can't move."

"Neither can I."

The knock came again.

"One of us has to get it," she whispered, sliding to his side and drawing the quilt to her chin. There was no doubt as to her choice.

Slanting her a punishing scowl, he untangled his legs from the sheets and pushed himself to his feet. He was halfway toward the door when, hearing Jordanna's gay laughter, he looked down.

The knock came a third time.

"Coming!" he yelled, racing toward the bathroom, returning as he pulled on one of the terry robes that had hung on a hook. "Pretty funny, huh?" he mumbled, then stopped before the door, donned his most composed expression and reached for the knob.

From her position of maximum concealment, Jordanna watched the waiter who wheeled in their dinner. She was instantly grateful that a young, innocent country girl hadn't been sent. Patrick looked far too appealing with his long, tanned legs extending far below the white robe, whose belt loosely ringed his hips. But, no, the waiter was very definitely a he, and though his tender age suggested he was perhaps as innocent as that country girl might have been, he was obviously well trained. If he suspected what he'd so inopportunely interrupted, he made no show of it. Rather, head bent to his task, he deftly transformed the tray on wheels into a table replete with fresh flowers and the finest of linen and china, not to mention a feast whose aroma was tantalizing.

When the young man left and they were alone once again, Jordanna threw back the quilt and scrambled from the bed. She was suddenly ravenously hungry. Returning quickly to the bathroom, Patrick produced a second robe, held it out for her as though it was the finest of furs, then bent to nip her ear. "I'd let you eat naked, but I don't think I'd make it." He glanced down as she lifted the first of the heavy metal covers. "On second thought, man cannot live by sex alone. That steak looks great!"

Jordanna had the good grace to set up his meal before uncovering her own. Then they ate greedily, all else forgotten. By the time they were done, nothing edible remained on the table.

Smacking his lips, Patrick sat back in the cushioned chair. "Think we should try the flowers? If they're half as good as the cake was—"

Jordanna's groan interrupted him. Hauling herself back on the lounge, she stretched out and crossed her ankles. "I'm stuffed. Nothing like pigging out."

He sent her a meaningful glance. "We seem to be doing a lot of that lately." As if suddenly endowed with an excess of energy, he bounded up, collapsed the sides of the table and pushed the whole thing out into the hall. When he returned, he gestured with his hand. "Move over."

Innocently she looked to either side of her. "Move over?"

"Make room for me."

"Here? What's wrong with your chair?"

"It's lonely. Come on." Swooping down, he lifted her, sank back into the lounge, then fitted her to his side. She had to admit that there was something very nice about being squashed by Patrick Clayes.

"Better?" she asked, looking up at him.

"Much. Are you okay?"

"Fine."

"Like more coffee? I could order—"

"Nothing. I'm really filled."

"How about an afterdinner drink. Brandy? Port?"

She shook her head. "Nothing, thanks." Closing her eyes she snuggled closer. "Pat?"

"Mmm?"

"Tell me about your career."

"My work?"

"Football."

He went still for a minute. She felt him looking down at her and tipped her head back.

"You don't really want to hear about that."

"I do." The truth was that she felt open enough, mellow enough to want to know everything about him

He saw the message in her eyes, the peace there. And he began quietly. "I played through junior high and high school, well enough to get a scholarship to college."

"Had you always intended to turn pro?"

"Uh-huh. Football had been my life from way back when." She nodded, recalling what he'd told her before. "Actually, I'd intended to win the Heisman Trophy. Needless to say, I didn't." Again, she nodded. She knew very well who had won it that particular year.

"No loss," she quipped. "It's only a piece of sculpted metal, and it's a bitch to dust."

Patrick snorted, then grew pensive. "Still, I wanted it. I'll never forget that day in November. I knew there were three of us in the running. According to my agent, I had the east sewed up. Peter had the west. Doug Shoenbrunn had the south. I waited and waited in that office for word, praying that I'd get it, convincing myself that I deserved it. Finally, I just went home. It was two in the morning when my agent called. I was devastated."

"It meant that much?"

"In dollars and cents, not to mention prestige. Almost like an Oscar for an actor. Thank God I didn't have to be on camera when they opened the envelopes. The presentation dinner was bad enough, but at least I'd had time to prepare myself for the loss. It was a blow, I'll tell you. And a harbinger. The following spring, Kirkland was the first player chosen in the draft. I wasn't picked until the third round."

"Why the discrepancy?"

"Go ask 'em. I'd led my team in back-to-back Cotton Bowl appearances and had the best passing record in the NCAA. Who knows what those guys base their decisions on? I sure as hell don't!"

Jordanna could feel the frustration oozing from him and momentarily regretted having raised the issue at all. By way of comfort, she slid a hand inside his robe and lightly kneaded his chest. "You did well, though. Proved them wrong. How many Super Bowl rings do you have?"

Responding to her soothing caress, he lowered his voice. "Just one. The other two I lost to you-know-who."

Relieved at the hint of humor in his tone, she grinned. "I had to polish those too. They were almost as bad as the trophy."

"Polish them? The rings?"

"Uh-huh. He wanted them to gleam when he held them up, which he tended to do very often, if you recall."

"You bet I recall. How not to win friends and influence people. But, damn it, Peter had that charisma. He could do whatever he wanted and still come out smelling like a rose. The world loves a winner. I guess it's as simple as that."

"If the world's love is what you want."

"Mmm."

"And it's not what you want, is it?"

"Not in that sense. Sure, I want to be respected for what I do. I want to be rewarded for it. But with the world's adulation? Uh-uh. I guess I'm like you. What's important is what *I* think. I need self-respect. I want to be able to go to sleep at night feeling good and honest and proud. God only knows how Kirkland slept."

"Like a baby. Says something about his values, doesn't it?"

Patrick hugged her closer and Jordanna knew that he understood and agreed. "Guess so. Anyway, I had my day with football. I've got my MVP awards, my ring, my lame shoulder." She slid her hand to that spot as he went on. "And now it's done. I am grateful; football gave me what I wanted. By the time I retired, I had enough of a name and a kitty to go out and start my own business. It's challenging and rewarding. I'm pleased with it."

"Tell me more, Pat. Are you all alone at the top?"

"I've got three partners. They contribute everything to the group that I can't. In some ways, my story's like yours. I may have a college degree and a smattering of postgraduate business courses under my belt, but nothing like their MBAs from Harvard and Columbia. While I was tossing that crazy little ball around, they were scoring touchdowns on Wall Street. What with their know-how, my money and the additional backing I had access to, we formed the Houghton Group."

Jordanna's hand ceased its gentle massage of his shoulder. She levered herself up and stared back at him. "The Houghton Group? *You're* the Houghton Group?"

The corners of his lips quirked in humor at her expression of amazement. "Sure. It's no big deal."

"Patrick, the Houghton Group has to be *the* up-and-coming firm. I mean, I'm far from an expert when it comes to venture capitalism, but I do read. You name it—the *Wall Street Journal*, *Forbes*, the *Times*—you've had fantastic write-ups in each of them during the past year!" She looked away, puzzled. "Strange. I don't remember reading your name. I must have been skimming—"

"My name wasn't *in* all of the articles. It's the Houghton Group, angel, not the Clayes Group. I like it that way."

Amazed, but now at the extent of his modesty, she continued to stare at him. He was so different, *so different*.

"Does it matter?" he asked so softly that, lost in her thoughts, she didn't follow at first.

"Hmm?"

"Does it matter who I am and who I'm with?"

"Of course not. It's just...fascinating."

He seemed troubled then. "Am I more fascinating now that you know I'm with the Houghton Group?"

And she understood. With a gentle smile, she touched her fingers to his lips. "Yes, you're more fascinating, but not in the way you think. You're more fascinating because by rights you should be arrogant as hell. Yet you're not. *That* is fascinating. It's also very, very refreshing." Stretching, she replaced her fingertips with her lips and kissed him softly. Then she set her cheek against his chest and slid an arm around him. His own locked her there moments before he spoke.

"Refreshing enough to last until Sunday?"

Her heart skipped a beat. "Till Sunday?"

"You don't have to be back tomorrow."

"No."

"Then stay here with me until Sunday. Please. I'd like it very much."

A slow smile spread over Jordanna's face. More than ever before she felt she was her own woman, doing what she wanted, albeit on whim. "I'd like it too," she said softly. "Thank you."

7

PATRICK STOOD AT HIS WINDOW, looking down on Park Avenue. Behind him his desk was covered with papers. His secretary sat just outside his door waiting to type the letters he was supposed to have dictated into his machine the night before. But he hadn't dictated. He hadn't done much of anything except think of Jordanna. It seemed to have become a habit of his.

In the two weeks since they'd left New Hampshire, each in his or her own car headed toward his or her own life, he'd tried to immerse himself in his work. He hadn't been terribly successful. Now, as had happened so very many times, he thought back to that weekend. It had been a dream, wonderful and warm, filled with everything he ever imagined and more. Not that they'd strayed far from their room for two days. At first they'd had the excuse of their clothes; it hadn't been until late Saturday that the inn had returned everything washed and neatly folded or hung up. Even then, though, they'd chosen to wear the soft terry robes or, more often, nothing at all.

They'd talked and made love, ordered breakfast in bed and made love some more, had wine and cheese then talked and made love again, ordered dinner, talked, made love. And each time it was better. They'd become the dearest of friends, the most superb of lovers. It had been sheer hell to think of letting her go.

That Sunday, as the hours had passed, a subtle tension had arisen. Both had known what was coming. Their conversation, their lovemaking had taken on a more urgent quality. At last he'd been the one to put it into words.

"We've got something too good to ignore, angel. You know that, don't you?"

She'd looked at him soulfully and had silently nodded.

He'd gone on. "We both need time to think. Once we're back in the city, things will take on a different perspective. It's all been so beautiful here, but far removed from reality. We're going to have to think about us in that other context now."

Again she'd nodded, but her agreement had only fueled his frustration. He'd half wished she'd argued that it wouldn't make any difference, that what they had would exist wherever, that she loved him. But she hadn't argued. She was too sensible for that. She'd been through too much in her life, too much with Peter Kirkland to be blind to the drawbacks of a relationship with Patrick. She had to come to terms with everything if they were to have a chance as a couple in the real world. And he had to come to terms with things too.

Had he? He wasn't sure. All the brooding and debating that he'd done, that he continued to do, had convinced him of one thing. He loved Jordanna. She was everything he'd always wanted in a woman—warm and intelligent and exciting and independent—everything, with one exception. She'd been married to Peter Kirkland.

He couldn't seem to put that thought to rest. It haunted him, as he'd been haunted for so many years living in Kirkland's shadow. And he was furious at himself for being haunted. Too often he pictured Jordanna's naked body, the body he knew so well, in Peter Kirkland's arms, and something angry coiled within him. Then he would relent and want her all the more. If he loved Jordanna, there was no reason why he shouldn't call her, see her, even marry her. To hell with Peter. To hell with the snide remarks they were sure to get. To hell with the inevitable newspaper stories their relationship was bound to generate. To hell with the world.

But he cared. It bothered him. For his sake *and* Jordanna's. He wanted nothing to mar the beauty of what they'd found.

Had she found it as well? He thought so. Everything she'd said and done during that weekend attested to the fact. He thought back to the last time they'd made love. She'd been more abandoned than she'd ever been, using those soft lips of hers, those slender hands, that agile body to conquer every inch of his flesh. She'd said it in her actions. He thought. She loved him. He thought. But what if he thought wrong?

Turning from the window, he gave a harsh snort. And he thought waiting for the Heisman decision had been tough! Here his heart was at stake, and he was in agony.

HALFWAY ACROSS TOWN, high in her office overlooking Sixth Avenue, Jordanna stared at the papers spread wide on her desk. Hearing a light knock at her door, she looked up to see Sally Frank enter.

"Whaddya think?" Sally asked, expectation in the eyes that darted from Jordanna to the desk top and back. "Like 'em?"

Jordanna pushed herself back in her chair. "They're okay."

"Just okay?"

"I don't know, Sally." Jordanna frowned. "There's something missing. I can't put my finger on it. Some little bit of extra excitement...or promise...or...oh, I don't know."

Sally came to perch on the edge of the desk. "The art department's been working on them for weeks. I thought they were pretty good."

"They are."

"But?"

Jordanna shrugged and raised tired eyes to her friend. Sally had been with her from the start and was the best advertising vice-president she could have hoped for. "I just don't know." She looked off toward the window. "Maybe it's me. I'm not sure what I want."

Sally thought for a minute. "Why do I hear something deeper in that than this ad campaign?"

Jordanna looked back. "Do you?"

"Uh-huh. Come on, love. 'Fess up. What's bothering you?"

"Is something bothering me?"

Sally rolled her eyes. "Always answering a question with a question. Is that the prerogative of presidents, or is it just you being evasive?" Her tone gentled. "What is it, Jordanna? You've been off somewhere since you got back from that trip of yours."

"From Minneapolis?"

"Not from Minneapolis. That was last week and it was pure business. I'm talking about that supposed vacation of yours. You were to be rested and refreshed. Instead you only seem distracted."

"Do I?"

"Come on, Jordanna. This is me. Sally. Your old friend. The woman whose wedding you were maid of honor at. The woman whose kids are your godkids. The woman who cries in your tea every time she has a fight with her husband. What is it, love? *Something*'s bothering you."

Jordanna looked at her for a minute, then pushed

herself from her chair and walked to the window. Perhaps she needed to talk, to share her thoughts with someone who might be able to help. Lord knew she'd come up with few enough answers on her own.

"I met someone."

"Someone. A man?"

"Mmm."

"Where?" Sally's enthusiasm flared. For years she'd been encouraging Jordanna to date, with far too little success.

"On the trip."

"In New Hampshire? You're kidding!"

"I wish I were."

"Why so glum? I think that's great! So what if he lives somewhere else. You're as mobile as most women nowadays." When Jordanna continued to gaze out the window, Sally bridled her tone. "Uh-oh. He's married."

"No."

"He's a punk-rock superstar?"

Jordanna managed to chuckle. "No."

"Then what? What could be so awful about a man you'd meet?"

"His name is Patrick Clayes."

"Nice name. Good strong sound."

Slowly Jordanna turned. "Doesn't it ring a bell?"

Sally frowned. "No. Should it?"

Slumping down onto the broad windowsill, Jordanna propped herself on a hand by either hip. "It would if you were into sports."

"I'm not. You know that."

"Norman would know the name."

"You bet Norman would know the name. He's a lost cause. Every weekend now it's football. Collegiate games on Saturdays, pro games on—uh-oh. Tell me, Jordanna. Who is Patrick Clayes?"

Jordanna took a deep breath, then let it out with a

huff. "Patrick Clayes is—was the quarterback who rivaled Peter for years."

"Ahh. Patrick Clayes."

"You *have* heard of him?"

"No. But I'll take your word that he is who he is. And I take it that bothers you."

"Yes. No. God, I don't know!"

Slipping from the desk, Sally joined Jordanna on the sill. She spoke very softly. "I've never seen you like this, love. Even when things are at their worst here, you're cool. You've always got an opinion, not that I've always agreed with you." When Jordanna sent her a scowl, she got back on the track. "This Patrick Clayes got to you, did he?"

"Yes."

Sally sat back. "There. Now we're getting somewhere. Want to tell me about it?"

"Not really."

"But you will."

"I guess I have to. I don't know what to do about it myself. And you're right. It's affecting my work."

Sally patted her hand. "Okay. Start at the beginning. I take it he was a member of the expedition."

In as few words as possible, Jordanna told her story. By the time she'd finished, Sally had much to consider. "You parted...just like that?"

"Just like that. It was the only way. He was right. We were living in a dreamworld."

"But I don't understand why it can't be a real world as well."

"Sally, the man is a football player."

"*Was* a football player."

"Same difference. Do you have any idea what I feel in my gut every time I remember what it was like being married to Peter?"

"Patrick's not Peter. You said it yourself. You kept expecting him to be that way, but he wasn't. He was kind and good and giving." She hesitated. "You're in love with him, aren't you?"

"Yes."

"Does he love you?"

"He didn't say that. All he said was that we'd have to try to cope with our relationship in the context of the real world." She looked at her friend beseechingly. "Don't you see, Sal? He fought being second banana to Peter all those years. How could he possibly become involved with me? I was Peter's wife."

"Sounds like he's already involved with you."

Jordanna quickly waved the argument aside. "That was *there*. We were in isolated circumstances. In a kind of limbo. It was like an island fling or...or a shipboard romance."

"But you love him."

"Yes!"

"And you want him to call."

Defeated, Jordanna lowered her head. "One part of me says no. That part of me wishes I'd never met him. I was happy with my life. It was uncomplicated." When Sally snorted, she specified. "In the personal sense, I mean. But...."

"The other part...."

"The other part of me feels empty. It wants to see him. Yes, damn it, it wants him to call."

"Why don't you call him?"

"I can't. I...I need time."

"The hell you do. Nothing is accomplished with you sitting here in this office and him—" she swung her hand "—out there somewhere."

"Park Avenue," Jordanna murmured. "His office is on Park Avenue."

"Then that's half the battle. You know where he is. So call him."

"I can't."

"Why not? Hell, you're aggressive enough around

here. You wouldn't blink an eyelash at the thought of picking up that phone and getting the president of Neiman-Marcus on the line."

"That's different."

"It doesn't have to be."

"It does. The president of Neiman-Marcus hasn't been batted around for years by Willow Enterprises."

"You didn't bat Patrick around. Peter did it."

"But I was married to Peter! And the world knows that."

Sally surged to her feet. "Screw the world, Jordanna Kirkland. You've never been one to make decisions based on what the world thought. You've made decisions based on what you thought was right. Call him. Pick up the phone and call him."

"No! I want him to call *me*!"

"Ahh. The ultimate fantasy." Sally's voice was gentle, as were the hands she placed on her friend's shoulders. "You, Jordanna Kirkland, are an old-fashioned girl at heart. I should have seen it sooner—the way you cry at weddings, the way you insist I take the day off when one of the kids has a birthday, the way you send champagne on anniversaries. You're a romantic. Even your marriage to Peter was that way at the start, wasn't it?"

"Yes."

"But you've grown cynical."

"Cautious."

"Whatever. And because the present fairy tale has a little glitch in it, you're willing to throw it away?"

"I never said that. All I said was that there were problems that I didn't know how to solve."

Sally shook her head, a sad smile on her face. "I wish I had the solutions, love, but I don't. You and Patrick are the only ones who can find them, but you've got to get together."

"I know," Jordanna whispered.

"He'll call."

"How can you be so sure? Maybe he's decided that fighting one Kirkland was enough."

"He's not going to fight you. He's going to fight *for* you."

"How can you be so sure?"

"Because I know you, Jordanna. I've seen the spell you cast over people. If Patrick Clayes spent that delicious weekend with you, he's hooked. And besides, I'm a romantic at heart myself. It'll work out. You'll see."

"I wish I could be as confident as you are." She pouted. "I'm not even sure that I *want* it to work out."

"You do. I can see it in your eyes. Don't forget, I've known you for nearly ten years now. I was with you in the aftermath of your divorce. I've been with you through years of occasional dates. And I've never seen you this way before. You do love him. And love is a stronger force than some stupid rivalry between little boys."

Jordanna laughed. Though Sally's conviction was subjective at best, she did feel better for the sharing of her woes. "Little boys. Stubborn little boys."

"Jealous little boys." Sally's eyes suddenly widened. "Hey, Craig doesn't know any of this, does he?"

"Lord, no! And I don't want him to know. Any of it. Got that, Sally?"

Sally turned an imaginary key at her lips. "Got it." Her eye skipped back to the ad mock-up on Jordanna's desk. "Now, about this campaign...."

THE AD CAMPAIGN was the last thing on Jordanna's mind when, two weeks later, she received a call from Alexander Shane. Drawn from her reverie concerning another call, one she had not received, she was slightly off balance.

"Alexander Shane?" she echoed when her secretary buzzed her to announce the call. "Of the Widener Corporation?"

"That's what he said."

Jordanna had heard of Alexander Shane *and* his Widener Corporation. In the past three years, the corporation had made headlines any number of times. She cringed at the reason.

"Put him on," she instructed, then straightened in her chair. A gravelly voice came on the line.

"Mrs. Kirkland?"

"Yes."

"This is Alexander Shane."

"Yes, Mr. Shane. How are you?" It was a formality. Her mind was already jumping ahead.

"Fine, thank you. I want to congratulate you. Willow Enterprises is doing quite well."

"Thank you. We believe it is."

"The Widener Corporation *knows* it is. Which is why I'm calling. We'd like to make you an offer."

Jordanna's heart began to thud. "An offer?"

"Yes. A merger. Willow Enterprises and the Widener Corporation."

Stunned, Jordanna cleared her throat. "I'm sorry, Mr. Shane, but we're not looking to merge with anyone, particularly a corporation that deals almost exclusively in electronics and defense gadgetry."

"Actually," came the other voice, undaunted, "we've expanded in recent months. You're aware of our takeover of Grossner Foods?"

Takeover. The word sent a frisson of fear through Jordanna. She gripped the phone more tightly. "Yes. I read about that. But what possible interest could you have in Willow Enterprises? We're still verv young—"

"You've got six plants spread across the country. Your profit margin has steadily increased. And, as the deal with Grossner Foods shows, we've begun to diversify."

More like trying to soften the image, Jordanna mused angrily. "I'm sorry, Mr. Shane. We're simply not interested."

"Is that a definite no?"

"Very much so," she said. Her pulse raced. Her eyes were glued to her desk. She waited.

Then it came. "In that case, I'd like to inform you that tomorrow morning we'll be filing a statement of intent with the Securities and Exchange Commission. Ads will be run in the major papers. A direct-mail offer will be made to your stockholders."

Shocked, Jordanna couldn't seem to catch her breath. She looked frantically around her office as though somewhere the proper words to quash this demon lay hidden.

"Well?" Alexander Shane prodded. "No response, Mrs. Kirkland?"

His smugness was enough to snap her from verbal paralysis. "My response, Mr. Shane, remains the same." She swallowed hard. "Willow Enterprises will not become a subsidiary of your organization."

"You may not have much choice. We've already bought up a substantial amount of your stock, and our tender offer will be for forty-eight dollars a share. As you know, that's ten above the market—"

"I know what the market price is," Jordanna cut in, blood boiling, "and I believe we have little left to say to each other. If you wish a friendly takeover, I'm afraid you'll have to go elsewhere. I'll fight, Mr. Shane. I haven't spent the past ten years of my life working to build a business, only to have it taken over by a warmongering conglomerate!"

Her caller only laughed. "It's that very spirit of

yours that has made Willow Enterprises so successful, Mrs. Kirkland. We're fighters. All of us. We'll
look forward to a successful union.''

Over my dead body, Jordanna fumed, hanging up
the phone and gripping the edges of her desk for
dear life. "This is incredible. Absolutely incredible."
Her eyes were wide, panic filled. "They can't do
this!" she wailed to no one at all. "They can't just
call up and steal my baby from under my nose! It's
not fair! *It's not fair!*"

Bolting from her chair, she began to pace the
room, only to return to her desk with a rush and lift
the phone. "Leila, get Tom Cherwin on the line."
Tom was vice-chairman of her board of directors
and a practicing lawyer.

Unfortunately, he wasn't much help. "It's perfectly legal, Jordanna. You know that as well as I do.
Widener has every right to attempt a takeover. At
least we know they haven't got too much stock; we
would have to have been notified otherwise. All we
can do is work fast."

"A board meeting tomorrow?"

"If possible. I do know that Margery Dodd is out of
town. Henry Walker may be too. If we have to let it go
another day, we can. Try to reach everyone else."

Jordanna's mind was reeling. She was amazed she
could sit still. But then there was this god-awful
quaking of her knees.

"I will. Tom, what are our chances?"

"Of emerging with things exactly as they've been
for the past few years? Next to nil." He paused, then
spoke very quietly. "Damn it, I never dreamed this
would happen. Fortunately, we have a clause in our
corporate contract to the effect that any change in
the status of the company has to be approved at a
meeting of the stockholders. Arranging such a meeting will take time. If Widener has borrowed money

to finance the acquisition, time for them may be at a premium."

"Their ads will be in the papers tomorrow. What if they manage to buy up enough of our stock to swing the vote?"

"We've got to prevent that. Get on the phone, Jordanna. You, personally. Call the largest of the block stockholders and explain what's happened."

"Damn it, Tom. Widener's offering forty-eight. It's an attractive deal. We can't match that."

"We'll have to. Somehow. I'd suggest a leveraged buy-out, borrowing money ourselves to buy back the stock and go private, but that'd put us on shaky ground financially." He paused. "There's always the chance of finding a friendly buyer."

"But I don't want to sell! Willow Enterprises is my life!"

"Which is why a friendly merger may be the only answer. If Widener takes us over, you and I and the board as we know it are bound to go, not to mention the greater part of your executive force. I don't care what Shane says on the phone about working together, I've seen how the man operates. He'll use us for his own ends. Don't tell me he's really interested in the welfare of the sportswoman. Hell, his fancy heat-seeking missiles could blow her away in a minute."

"You're supposed to be making me feel better, Tom," Jordanna scolded. "Let's not worry about heat-seeking missiles for the time being. Let's concentrate on keeping the guy's finger off our button, okay?"

"Sorry, Jordanna. Damn. We should have clauses to protect management."

"Why don't we?"

"Because we never thought in terms of being taken over before."

They were wasting valuable time. "Well, we are now. Listen, I'm going to start making some of those calls. I want to reach as many of the major stockholders as possible before Widener's ad hits the papers. What do I tell them?"

"Tell them to hold off while we look into counteroffers."

"Right." She was furiously scribbling notes. "And the board of directors—I'll call Marge and Henry first. If they can't make it until Thursday morning, we'll meet then."

"Fine. In the meantime, let me get an analyst on it. If we're going to need a white knight, we'd better get on the stick."

White knight. Jordanna pondered the term, a common one in takeover jargon. In her mind's eye she pictured Patrick, and a pang of need joined those ones of desperation that filled her. More than ever she wanted to talk with him. He'd understand, give her encouragement and strength. But he hadn't called...and there were others she had to talk with now.

As she'd done so often in the past four weeks, as she'd done so often in the past ten years, she put her personal needs on hold.

JORDANNA SPENT THE ENTIRE DAY and much of the evening on the phone. She contacted each of the members of the board and set up a meeting for early Thursday morning. She called each of the major stockholders and made her plea for restraint. It was hard; without a concrete counteroffer, she was appealing to them on grounds of sheer loyalty. Fortunately, though money was the name of the game, those she spoke with appeared to be the loyal type.

She called each of the six plants across the country, explaining to her managers what had happened and enlisting their aid in convincing those of their employees who held stock not to sell. This task was somewhat easier. The employees of Willow Enterprises were treated well; a threat to the organization was a direct threat to their own well-being.

Between calls she met with her executive staff, all of whom were stockholders as well. It was from this group that she found the greatest support. Their fury at the takeover threat and determination that it wouldn't succeed was a source of encouragement.

Nonetheless, by the time she'd returned home and made calls to several stockholders she hadn't been able to reach earlier, she was totally drained. It was all she could do to stumble into bed, and then she tossed and turned fitfully until dawn, when she dressed and returned to the office to renew the campaign for survival.

By ten in the morning, she was exhausted and discouraged. When her secretary knocked on her door bearing a fresh cup of coffee, Jordanna slumped in her chair and gave a wan smile. "Thanks, Leila. I need this."

"How's it going?"

"Oh, who knows? You make the calls and put forth your case and then hope for the best." Setting the coffee to the side, she opened the *Wall Street Journal*. "Have you seen it?"

"Yes," Leila answered. "It's pretty awful, don't you think?"

"God," she said in a defeated tone, "I've seen so many ads like this, never imagining that one day Willow Enterprises would be the target. It seems so unreal." She slapped the page. "But there it is. In black and white. A tender offer that may be too sweet for some of our stockholders to resist. They've probably all seen it by now. I can imagine what other papers it's in."

"They'll stick by you, Jordanna. I know they will. You've been good to them. They can't ignore that fact."

"I'm hoping that's so. They've got to know that if Widener takes us over things will change. And I doubt for the better—"

The ring of the phone from beyond the door broke into her words. With a quiet, "Excuse me," Leila ran back to her desk to answer it.

"Take a message!" Jordanna called after her. "Have them call back in ten minutes! I need a break!" She watched Leila slip into her chair and lift the receiver, then turned off thought of who it might be. Coffee cup in hand, she walked to the window.

She felt tired, so tired. And very, very empty. Things had happened so fast. It seemed hard to believe that a mere twenty-four hours before she'd been so innocent. Willow Enterprises had been hers then.

Tom had been right. With Alexander Shane's call, things had changed irrevocably. They would never quite return to the old status quo, Jordanna knew. And facing the loss of her company, she was suddenly less adverse to the thought of a compromise solution.

For an instant she imagined what would happen if she did lose. The business was her life. She had nothing else. Nothing...but dreams.

And he hadn't called.

Setting her coffee cup on the sill when her hand began to shake, she pressed her fingers to her mouth. Even before all this had happened, she'd felt empty. There was only one man who could fill that emptiness, and he was—

"Jordanna?"

Certain she'd only imagined his voice, she closed her eyes against the sting of tears.

"Jordanna?"

This time the voice was closer, very familiar, very dear. And real. Turning sharply, hand still pressed to her mouth, she focused through misty eyes on the man she'd missed so desperately for the past four weeks. She tried to say his name, but her lips only made the movements.

Patrick walked steadily forward, his heart pounding at the simple sight of her. He felt her anguish, had felt it the instant he'd opened the paper that morning. And suddenly who she was hadn't mattered, whose wife she'd been, who saw. He'd had to come. He needed to be there for her.

When he was a hand's width away, he stopped. He had his needs. But what about hers? What if she didn't want to see him, particularly at this time? He saw the pain in her eyes, the glimmer of tears. And he thought he'd die if he couldn't help her.

The tears welled higher, then began to trickle one by one down her cheeks. He was about to reach out and smooth them away when Jordanna swayed toward him. Then she was in his arms, clinging as tightly to him as he was to her. And the waiting was over.

"Ahh, angel," he crooned, hugging her as she wept softly. "Shh. It's all right. Everything's going to be all right now."

She didn't argue. She couldn't. Somehow, in Patrick's embrace, she believed it for the first time. The conviction was irrational. Emotional. She knew it, but that didn't matter. Things had indeed taken on a different perspective.

"Oh, Pat," she whispered, when at last she was able to speak, "I'm so glad you're here."

His arms trembled as he held her tighter. "I've been wanting to come. You have no idea how much. But I was afraid. Of so many things. Then, when I saw Widener's notice this morning, those other things didn't seem to matter anymore. I love you,

Jordanna. I want to be here. I want to help. I know how much Willow Enterprises means to you."

But she was shaking her head against his cheek. "I love you too, Pat. I'm glad you're here. So glad you're here."

He held her face then, brushing at her tears with his thumbs. His gaze adored her, reacquainting itself with each of her features as though it had been years rather than weeks since he'd seen her last. When he kissed her, his lips spoke of the pent-up longing, the anguish that was hers, now theirs.

He smiled. "You've grown."

"I'm wearing heels."

"And a skirt and silk blouse and makeup."

Self-conscious, she ran a finger beneath her eye. "I must be a mess."

It was Patrick's turn to shake his head. "You look beautiful. Very chic and sophisticated. Of course, I still like the way you look totally bare."

She smiled for the first time in more than twenty-four hours, and rubbed her forehead against his chin. "You men are all the same. One-track minds, all of you."

"No, angel," he murmured gently. "I love you the way no man ever has or ever will. I've been a fool to wait this long to tell you. These past four weeks I've been surviving on memory alone. But I need more now. You're warm and wonderful. The thought of you gives me life. You have no idea how much I admire you."

His words brought reality back with a thud. "Oh, Pat," she whispered, eyes filling again, "what am I going to do?"

Taking her under his wing, he guided her to the sofa on one side of her office. "You're going to relax, first of all. You look like you haven't slept in a week."

"It was really only a night. Funny how a takeover attempt can do that to a person."

They were sitting on the sofa, knees touching as they faced each other. Patrick took her hands in his.

"It's so awful, Pat. I mean, it never occurred to me that we'd run into trouble like this. Hostile offers are for other firms. Not Willow Enterprises. We were doing so well on our own. And I've poured so much of my life into this. If it's taken away, I don't know what I'll do!"

"It won't be taken away, angel. There are ways to fight."

"I know. But it's hard. And it costs." Pausing, she looked down. "Were you ever in a car accident, Pat?"

"A car accident?"

She raised her eyes. "I had one once. Not long after I got my license. There was a blind intersection. I never saw the car that hit me until well after I came to a stop crunched around a telephone pole." When Patrick winced, she was quick to assure him. "Oh, no one was hurt. But my car was totaled. There were police and insurance forms to fill out, the inconvenience of being without a car, not to mention the money to shell out for the new car that the insurance didn't quite cover. I kept thinking that none of it would have happened if I'd been ten seconds faster or slower. I kept wanting to turn back the clock, to replay the scene and have everything bad go away."

Her shoulders slumped and she focused on Patrick's hands, so strong in hers. "I feel that way now, only I don't know what I could have done differently. A day ago, none of this was happening. Now, suddenly, my business—my sweat and tears—is up for grabs. I want to turn back the clock, but I can't."

"No, you can't. Life isn't that way. But you're not unique in wishing it, angel. It's a normal feeling for someone in your position. I know. I've had any number of friends go through the same thing."

"How did they handle it?"

"The first thing they had to do was to accept the fact that they couldn't turn back the clock. That accomplished, they sought the best possible solution to the problem."

Jordanna took a deep breath and let it out slowly. "The best possible solution. Right now, *anything* looks pretty bad."

"That's because you're still at stage one. It takes time."

"Just what we haven't got."

"But you've got people working on alternatives to a Widener takeover?"

"Oh, yes. And I've contacted most of the major stockholders. We're sending wires to the rest. The board's meeting tomorrow morning." She smiled sadly. "But I'm discouraged." As she looked at him, she found the respite she needed. "God, you look good." Freeing a hand from his, she stroked the side of his head. His hair was thick and rich. She dropped her gaze. "Pin-striped suit, crisp white shirt, dashing rep tie and these sprinkles of silver in your hair."

"Those are from thinking about you all month. Wondering. Worrying."

"Don't give me that. I saw those strands of gray last month in New Hampshire."

"They came from needing you all my life and not knowing who you were."

"You've got an answer for everything, don't you?" Slipping her arms inside his jacket, she leaned against him. He felt so solid, so strong. When his arms went around her back, she felt very, very safe.

"I may."

At his cautious tone, she tipped her head back. "What does that mean?"

"It means," he went on, taking a breath, "that I'd like to help you."

"You are helping me. You're here."

"More than that. I'd like to help you fight Widener." At her puzzled expression, he continued. "The best way to fight a hostile tender offer is to counter with an offer from a friendly source. I may just be able to provide that source."

Jordanna inched back, a frown on her face. "The Houghton Group?"

"Uh-huh. I've got investors just waiting for a good cause. This might be it."

"But... but you work with new ventures or businesses that need rebuilding. I didn't think you were into acquisitions."

"There's not much difference in the mechanics of it all. Just because we haven't made a name for ourselves in the takeover field doesn't mean we haven't dabbled in it. Right off the bat I can think of four major investors who would be interested in forming a group to back Willow Enterprises."

"How can you say that? I mean, you didn't know about any of this until the ad appeared in the paper this morning. You can't know much about us."

Patrick snickered. "Evidently you don't know much about the ways of boys. When they have their first big crush on a girl, they find out everything about her. Where she lives. What she likes to eat. What her favorite color is. What time she leaves for her piano lessons."

"I never took piano lessons," Jordanna whispered. "And this is a crush?"

"No, ma'am. No more than I'm still a boy. I'm a man. And in love. Which means that I haven't spent the past month just staring out a window." He smiled, a faint red tinge creeping above his collar. "Well, I guess I've done my share of that too. But I also did my homework. I read everything I could about Willow Enterprises. Between that and what you've told me yourself, I know that it'd be a sound investment, one I could recommend to any number of my clients."

She simply stared for a minute, then, dazed, shook her head. "Oh, Pat. I don't know...."

"Have you got another possible suitor?"

"No. Not yet."

"Then why not me...uh, my group?"

"Because I don't want to be bought, period!"

"You may not have much choice."

Stricken, she sat back. Alexander Shane had used identical words on the phone yesterday. Coming with such gentleness from Patrick, they had the ring of authenticity rather than spite. "No, I may not," she stated, sagging against the sofa.

"Would it be so terrible?"

"In that I'd lose control of my company, yes."

"But that wouldn't necessarily be the case. What if, between you and me personally, we held a majority of the shares?"

"I haven't got that kind of money!"

"But I do. Or at least I have access to it." He leaned toward her, propping an arm on the sofa back. "What if we included specific phrases in the contract that would assure your board control of the everyday workings of the company? What if we guaranteed that you would have sole authority over personnel? What if we took measures to assure that no other conglomerate such as Widener could possibly attempt a takeover?"

She thought about that for a minute. "Sounds idealistic."

"It's not. It can be done. Believe me, Jordanna. I know what I'm talking about."

That, too, she thought about. But it was all so sud-

den. Her mind seemed suddenly crammed to over-
flowing. "I don't know, Pat." She looked away.
"There are promises . . . and there are promises. Fancy
legal language can be as deceptive as anything else."

For the first time since he'd begun to set forth his
proposal, Patrick hesitated. "Jordanna?" His fingers
were firm as they turned her face toward him. "Do
you trust me?"

"When you look at me that way, how can I help it?"

"But *do* you trust me? I mean, really trust *me*?"

"Yes."

"Why?"

"Because I love you."

"And because you know that I love you? That I
would never do anything to hurt you?"

"Yes," she whispered. She found the urgency of
his expression to be as mesmerizing as his words.

When he stood, reached out and drew her up into
his arms, she went eagerly. "Then let me get to work
on it. Let me discuss it with my partners and see
what I can come up with."

"I have to talk with my people too."

"Of course you do. It'll take me a little time to put
something together anyway. In the meantime you
can tell them what I've told you." He smiled and
crushed her against him. "If anyone gets the short
end of the stick here, it's apt to be my investors. I
think I'd give you the world if I could. Ahh, Jordanna." A low growl came from deep in his throat
as he buried his face in her hair. "It's so good to hold
you."

"And you," she whispered, wrapping her arms
more tightly around his neck. Her lips were waiting
when he sought them and opened hungrily for his
kiss.

His hands released her only to slide along her
blouse in search of her breasts. He found them full

and warm, nipples responding instantly to his touch.

"Ahh. She wears a bra."

"I warned you."

"Mmm. I'm supposed to be thinking of putting together the deal of a lifetime and all I can think about is very slowly taking off every bit of this silky stuff from your body. You know what I'd do then?"

Suddenly and unbelievably high, she laughed. "What?"

He proceeded to whisper in her ear precisely what he'd do, and she went moist and quivery all over.

"When?" she countered with such urgent demand that it was Patrick's turn to laugh.

"How about tonight? Your place. Around nine?"

"Mmm. I'd like that. I live on—"

"I know where you live. A boy's crush, remember?" He pressed her to him a final time, leaving no doubt as to his very manhood, then, with reluctance, held her away. "Maybe I should pick you up here."

"No. I'll want to change and shower and…make myself presentable."

"Now that really *is* funny," he said, popping a kiss on the tip of her nose before heading for the door. Halfway there, he stopped, turned, then retraced his steps and swept her into his arms a final time. "I love you, angel. I love you."

His kiss echoed the words, to be echoed in turn by Jordanna's responding lips. It was with great effort that they separated. Pat shook his head as he crossed the room once more. "Lots to do. Lots to do." Then, without turning, he slammed a fist against a palm and threw his head back. "Wow, do I feel great!"

The only thing that was missing was a clicking of heels in the air. Jordanna watched him go, a look of loving indulgence on her face. When she was alone once more, she realized that, remarkably, she felt great too.

8

As THE DAY WORE ON, Jordanna's feeling of euphoria diminished only slightly. Buoyed by the knowledge that Patrick loved her even more than by the chance that he might have a solution for her woes, she felt in control of herself once again.

The influx of calls from worried brokers began. Though she'd known that the Widener ad would be read by many people, she had dared to hope that it wouldn't cause an immediate stir. For the most part, the calls she received were positive. There were those, however, that were tentative, others that were downright dubious.

Between calls she thought of Patrick, and her spirits inevitably rose.

When she called Tom Cherwin and told him of a potential suitor in the Houghton Group, he was more than pleased. The group was honest and well-respected, he told her quite unnecessarily. Though his analyst had already sniffed out several potential buyers, Tom promised to call him immediately about the Houghton addition.

With what was left of the day, Jordanna put her thoughts together for the board meeting to be held early the next morning. Several well-placed phone calls gave her valuable information on the Widener Corporation, which she proceeded to organize for presentation at the meeting. Though she had every reason to believe that the board would vote down the merger, she wanted to take no chances. Along with her notes on Widener, she gathered the latest figures on Willow Enterprises. After handing the lot to Leila for typing, she returned to her desk to take care of the routine work she'd been neglecting for two days.

It was well after eight when she finally turned out the lights and left the deserted office behind to begin the healthy twenty-minute walk home. Head high, she welcomed the brisk December breeze. She felt tired but exhilarated, and more excited with each step. It amazed her that Patrick's reappearance in her life could make such a difference; whether the Houghton Group could indeed come through for her seemed secondary to the fact that, where emptiness had existed before, now there was a rich bouquet of hope. The knot that twisted in her stomach each time she thought of Widener's bid seemed that much easier to bear.

Fifth Avenue was alive with lights, made all the more gay by the approach of Christmas. Wrapping her cashmere scarf more tightly around the collar of her coat, Jordanna turned down Seventy-eighth Street with a smile. Regardless of what tomorrow held, she was determined to enjoy tonight to the fullest. *He loved her.* What a wonderful feeling!

Taking her front steps at a trot, she let herself into the lobby of the narrow brownstone, snaked her mail from its box, then took the elevator to the fourth floor. Moments later, with steaks removed from the freezer and put in the microwave to defrost, a head of Boston lettuce rinsed and left to drain, and potatoes put on to boil in preparation for an au gratin casserole, she dashed upstairs to quickly shower.

With the freshest bit of makeup skillfully applied, she slid into a pair of dark velvet pants, a white silk blouse that billowed at the sleeves, and strappy black leather high-heeled sandals. A bright sash of red silk completed the outfit. After sending a brush through her mercifully wash-and-wear hair and spraying her pulse points with cologne compliments of Oscar de la Renta, she raced back to the kitchen to drain the potatoes, slice them and layer them with onions and gruyere. Then she stuck the casserole in the oven while she went to work on the salad. She was in the process of fluting a cucumber when her buzzer rang.

Nine o'clock on the dot. He was prompt. But then, had she expected otherwise? Had she *wanted* otherwise? With a smug smile, she wiped her hands on a paper towel and headed for the intercom by the door.

"Hello?" She knew she was beaming, and she hoped she sounded less giddy than she felt. Given the threat to the business, it seemed indecent that she should feel so light-headed, but she couldn't help it.

"Room service," came the deep voice she'd recognize, fuzzy intercom or no.

"It took you long enough," she teased.

"I'm right on time!"

"Four weeks late. I just hope everything's still hot."

"Oh, it's hot, all right. And getting hotter." The voice lowered. "Damn it, Jordanna, buzz me in. One of your neighbors just walked by and gave me the strangest look."

Laughing, she pressed the button, waited until she was sure he'd have cleared the door before releasing it, then went into the hall to wait for the elevator to arrive.

The doors slid open with a soft hum. Arms laden with bundles, Patrick turned sideways to see her. She reached forward and drew him out, then scowled.

"That's quite a load. It's a miracle you haven't tripped and spilled the goodies. Then where would we be?"

"Depends on which goodies you're worried about," he drawled, taking a broad look around him as, led firmly by Jordanna, they entered her duplex. "Hey, this is nice!"

Not quite forward enough to start grabbing for the bundles he carried, one of which was very obviously from a florist, Jordanna clasped her hands before her and joined his inspection. "I like it. I've been here for five years now. The rooms are narrow, but that seems to be a regional hazard. The fellow who lived here before me took most of the walls down, so the place looks larger. And what with upstairs and down, it's plenty roomy."

"I can see."

What Patrick saw was a vision of impeccable style. Thick rugs carpeted the floors. Beautifully upholstered chairs and a love seat comfortably filled the living area, and an exquisite marble-topped dining table and four straight chairs drew the eye on. Sculpted pieces, each unique and of varied materials, rested upon coffee tables and a small oak buffet. Original oils hung on the walls. The overall color scheme was a blend of cream and powder blue.

"Classy. Like you," he said in soft appreciation, then turned to face her and raised his voice in imitation of a door-to-door salesman. "And for the classy lady, we have—" he juggled his bundles and began handing them to her one by one "—flowers... wine...ice cream...and—" he cleared his throat as he passed her the two largest packages "—a little something for later."

"For later?"

"Mmm. Not to be opened now." He shrugged out

of his topcoat and tossed it onto the nearest chair, then retrieved the two large boxes from Jordanna, dropped them near his coat and went for the ice cream and wine. "These have to be stashed," he said, heading for the kitchen with such ease that Jordanna half suspected he'd researched the layout of her apartment as well. She followed, gently cradling the flowers, pleased that he should feel at home here.

"Pat?" Her voice held a touch of unsureness, hinting at the crisis that had brought him to her office that morning.

Having already deposited the ice cream in the freezer, he closed the refrigerator door on the wine, turned and put a finger against her lips. "Shh." Then he took her hand and began walking. "Put the flowers down. I want to see the rest of the place."

She barely had time to deposit the wrapped bunch on the table before she was swept back through the dining room and living room to the stairs. Her senses had already begun to quiver. All day she'd been excited about seeing Pat, yet the reality was so much better than the anticipation that it took every bit of her self-command to call his name again.

"Pat? What about—"

"The deal?" He was taking the carpeted steps two at a time. Jordanna had to trot to keep up. "It's looking good." He poked his head into the first room he reached. "A study. Nice. Do you do much work at home?" Already he was dragging her on.

"Yes. I try to bring papers—"

"Ah, angel. This is you." He was at the second room, clearly the one he sought. Tightly holding her hand, he took in every inch of the room, from the lacquered dresser and dressing table, both of which matched the carpet perfectly, to the single modern oil on the wall, to the pale-blue-covered bed. With the gentle pull of his hand, he brought her to him.

His dark brown eyes suddenly saw nothing but her. "Have I told you tonight how much I love you?"

"You haven't told me much of anything," she complained, but it was in a whisper and there was the faintest smile on her face to say that those three little words were the only ones she really needed to hear at the moment.

"I love you," he murmured, taking her face in his hands. His lips brushed her eyes, closing them, then her nose and her cheeks before settling at last on her mouth in a kiss filled with need and purpose. "Mmm, do you taste good." He raised his head only to focus on the buttons of her blouse.

It didn't matter to Jordanna that she'd dressed mere moments before. She'd dressed for him. Perhaps simply to be *un*dressed by him. Without hesitation, she slipped her hands beneath his jacket.

"You changed." In place of the gray pin-striped suit was a navy blazer and gray-flannel slacks.

He was down to the third button of her blouse and proceeding steadily. "I keep things at the office." He bent his head to lick her neck as she slid the blazer from his arms. "When I want to freshen up, it's easier than going home. And since I had to work late...."

She loosened his tie and worked at the knot. "No wonder you had to work late. You must have spent half the day shopping. Flowers. Wine. Ice cream. Ice cream?"

"Rum raisin." He untied the bow of her sash. "I get this craving sometimes."

"What's in the boxes?" The knot at his neck came free. She tugged off his tie and tossed it aside, then began on his shirt buttons as he pulled her blouse from her pants.

"That's a surprise. I told you. For later." Pushing the blouse from her shoulders, he had her momentarily manacled. His mouth found the soft swell of her breast, just above the lace of her bra, and moistly kneaded the burning flesh.

"Pat!"

At her hoarse cry, he freed her arms of their silken bonds. The truth was that while he wanted to take things slowly, that was a pipe dream. He needed to feel her hands on him. Needed that desperately. He tugged his shirttails free while she worked feverishly at the last of his buttons. She smoothed the fabric to the side just as he unhooked her bra. Then they were kissing again, hands touching each other, and he was crushing her bare breasts against his chest, feeding on her excitement as she fed on his.

Suddenly time was of the essence. The only thing that seemed to matter was that they be naked, together, joined. Jordanna fumbled with his belt, then thrusting it aside, pulled at his zipper. Patrick nearly tore the button from her waistband in his effort to free her from her velvet pants. For several minutes, then, confusion reigned. It was a question of whose hands were supposed to be doing what where. Their pants, both pairs, hit the floor only after a bit of contorting. The scene was indeed comical. Between kisses they laughed, then renewed the farce.

But it wasn't a farce, because the outcome was breathtaking. There seemed no crisis more critical than the affirmation of their love on this most physical of planes. Swept into the immediacy of an overpowering need, Jordanna was aware of nothing but Patrick. Whereas moments before she'd had every intention of wheedling business news from him, now she could only think of her need to possess and be possessed by the magnificent man her frenzied hands had laid bare.

Both naked, they fell down to the bed. Lips met, tongues dueled. Made for each other, their bodies meshed so naturally that Patrick was inside her before she could begin to catch her breath.

There was no turning back from the fierce need that gripped them. It was as though, given the urgency of all else in their lives, they had to speak that much louder of their personal bond.

"I love you. I love you." Patrick murmured the words again and again. Jordanna simply arched higher to receive him, to give everything she had in return. Their shared adoration put their joining in that much more exalted a sphere, so that when the final moment of joy seized them, it was that much stronger, that much sweeter, that much more soul-reaching than it had ever been before.

"Angel...oh, God!" he gasped, collapsing on top of her. She could barely breathe, but just then she would have given her very life for him if he asked. "That was phenomenal!"

Eyes closed, she wrapped her arms as tightly as she could around his back. Her blissful smile spoke of her agreement as her vocal cords could not. When she remained silent, Patrick raised his head, looked down at her, then quickly slid to her side. She followed him over until they lay nose to nose.

"I love you," she whispered, combing her fingers through his hair. His brow was damp; she stroked it with her thumb.

"Do you? Do you really?" He'd had all day to assimilate the words, yet he couldn't hear them enough. Somehow he sensed it would always be that way.

"Uh-huh."

"When did you decide?"

"I'm not quite sure. I knew something was up when we left New Hampshire. The drive home was dismal. Then when I got back here, all I could do was picture you in this bed." She inhaled deeply, loving the scent that was uniquely his, and eyes moist, she shook her head in amazement. "I can't believe you're here. You came when I needed you most. Thank you."

"Don't thank me, angel. I needed you just as badly." It was his turn to look amazed. "It's odd how things happen."

"Does it bother you still ... my having been married to Peter?"

"Not the way it did. Knowing that you need me helps. I don't think I'll ever be able to forgive him for trying to subjugate you the way he did. You've got so much to offer. A man would be totally selfish to try to curb that. Part of what I love about you is your commitment to Willow Enterprises."

For the first time since Patrick had arrived, Jordanna felt that now familiar knot form in her stomach. "You do think you can come up with something to save us?"

"I'm sure I can. Two of my partners are interested, and among us we've got eight clients who are as enthusiastic. I'll make more calls tomorrow. In the meantime, our lawyers are working on preliminary contracts. What I need from you now are figures." He hesitated. "Do you think our man could take a look at your books?"

"Of course! That is, it's okay with me. I'll raise it with the board tomorrow. I'm sure they'll approve if you can guarantee us confidentiality."

"Done."

"Oh, Pat," she breathed, draping an arm around his neck. "Do you really think it would work? With the clauses you mentioned?"

"I don't see why not. You've got a solid organization. None of us wants to change that. The investors would be getting something good. How can they complain?"

"The price would have to be high, at least higher than Widener's offer."

"I know that, but we'll pay. It'll come back tenfold in time."

"What if Widener ups its bid?"

"We'll counter it. Trust me, angel. It'll work. You'll see. It'll work." He paused then, sniffing the air. "Is something burning?"

"Oh no! My casserole!" Within instants, Jordanna was out of bed and flying down the stairs, muttering frantic thoughts about scorched gruyere cheese. Wearing nothing but a pair of oven mitts, she removed the dish from the heat and set it atop the stove.

"Did it survive?" Patrick asked from behind, staring over her shoulder at the crisp crust of what was supposed to have been a delicately browned accompaniment to the steaks, which lay on the counter, and the lettuce, now slightly wilted nearby.

"I don't believe this," she wailed. "I wanted to impress you with my culinary skills."

"It looks...good."

"If you're looking for something to gnaw on." She let out a long breath, then couldn't help but grin. "Well, at least you can't say I didn't try."

Patrick turned her around and clasped his hands at the small of her back. "I didn't expect you to be a cook. As a matter of fact, I had quite a different impression."

Her thoughts joined his in recollection of their first dinner on the trail in New Hampshire. "I never said I didn't cook. The guys suggested that. I mean, for myself I rarely do much of anything. But I *can* do it when the occasion demands."

"This occasion *doesn't* demand it. I just wanted to be with you tonight. I couldn't give a damn about food."

"That was obvious," she mused aloud, but blushed when she realized that there was good reason her casserole had burned. She hadn't been paying it much heed herself. When she was in Patrick's arms, not much else seemed to matter.

"I tell you what," he began, setting her back and heading for the living room. "I'll give you a hand with dinner."

"I thought you weren't hungry."

"The sight of that steak just changed my mind." But he wasn't focusing on the steak. He was snapping the cords from the two large boxes he'd brought with him. Jordanna watched, growing more curious by the minute. A bright smile broke out on her face when, boxes emptied, he returned to her with one white terry robe slung over his arm and the other held open for her.

"I don't believe it." She shook her head, then laughed. Turning, she slid her arms into the awaiting sleeves. "You came prepared."

"It's winter. I didn't want you catching cold."

"Pretty sure of yourself, weren't you?" When she would have tied the belt, Patrick's hands were reaching around her to do it.

His lips brushed her ear. "You weren't exactly discouraging this morning. I'd never force myself on an unwilling woman."

"Never?" Jordanna teased, closing her hands over his and leaning back against his strength.

"Well, not unless she wanted me to."

"But then she wouldn't be unwilling."

"Unless that was her particular fantasy."

Jordanna turned in his arms then and looked gently up. "You are into fulfilling fantasies, aren't you?"

"I try."

Standing on tiptoe, she kissed him softly. "You do

well at it. I think it must be your forte. A professional white knight."

"They didn't call me Lance for nothing."

She recalled having said similar words to John, and smiled.

"What is it?" Patrick asked. He sensed her mind had wandered and was unwilling to let it go far.

Reaching for the robe on his elbow, she opened it and draped it around his shoulders. "I was just thinking of a discussion I had with John up in the woods. He's a nice guy. A philosopher, if mathematicians can be that. We were talking football."

"Oh?"

"Mmm. Funny, when I first saw you up there, I could only think of you as Lance. That changed pretty quick."

"Did it?" Patrick asked. His expression was suddenly serious. He'd wondered if it still bothered her that he had played football. She'd made it clear from the start that she had negative feelings about the game. And though she'd seemed to have come to accept that aspect of his past when they were in New Hampshire—hadn't she, herself, asked him all about it?—he'd had any number of fears that when they'd returned to New York those negative feelings might come to the fore. "How do you feel about it now?"

Jordanna knew precisely what he'd been thinking and, in hindsight, felt guilty for having made some of the statements she had. True, she was biased and, true, with good cause. But she'd generalized. She saw that now.

"I think," she began slowly, "that you gave the game a very important part of your life. I can only respect you for that. I also think that there's far more to you than football. You've left it behind. You're a successful businessman now. And a very nice human being."

His mouth took hers in a slow, savoring kiss. "Mmm. I guess I can live with that." Unable to resist the appeal of the lips he'd left soft and moist, he kissed her again. But his body was quickly responding to other soft, moist sources of appeal, and lest he repudiate Jordanna's compliment and prove himself nothing more than a rutting beast, he set her back, secured his robe tightly and straightened his shoulders. "Now—" he cleared his throat "—about those steaks...."

Grilled medium rare on the Jenn-Air, the steaks were delicious, as was the salad and, miraculously, the potatoes once the top crust had been scraped away. With a dozen aromatic long-stemmed roses gracing the center of the marble table and Patrick scooping the last of his rum raisin ice cream from its bowl, Jordanna sat back in amusement.

"You can lick it if you want."

His cheeks went red and he set his spoon down. "Sorry. I get carried away with this stuff."

She held up a hand. "Don't apologize. It's a delight watching a growing boy eat. As for me—" she patted her stomach "—I don't think I've eaten as much in...in...a month."

"Let me see." His hand pushed hers away and caressed her softness. "Mmm. You do feel stuffed. I think the best thing for you to do is to stretch out somewhere comfortable." He stood up.

"What did you have in mind? *Patrick...!*"

Lifting her in his arms, he started for the stairs. "The bed. Where else can one stretch out comfortably?"

JORDANNA AWOKE in the middle of the night in a cold sweat. Eyes wide in the darkness, she listened to those city sounds that never seemed to end. They were as they'd always been, but there was a new sound joining them. Patrick's breathing. Slow. Even.

She'd dreamed she was alone, but he was right beside her. Turning to face him, she moved her arm until it touched his. The feel of his flesh was comforting, the memory of his lovemaking intoxicating. But still there was the matter of her baby—Willow Enterprises—in danger. Unsettling, to say the least.

Over and over she reviewed the situation. It occurred to her that if the Widener Corporation had not attempted its takeover, Patrick might not have come to her when he had. In time he would have. She was sure of that. If only it hadn't taken this particular catalyst to bring them together!

Time and again she tried to imagine the future, but couldn't. Naive as she'd been, she'd never entertained thoughts of any kind of a takeover, let alone a hostile one. Despite what Patrick had said, she couldn't get past stage one; she simply couldn't seem to accept the fact that Willow Enterprises, against its will, was being forced to change its status. It was unfair and infuriating and not at all conducive to peace of mind.

Snuggling closer to Patrick's warmth, she closed her eyes and concentrated on how wonderful it was to be with him. But sleep was a long time in coming, and she was up again at first light, unable to sleep a minute longer.

Stealing softly from the bed, she pulled on her running gear, left a note for Patrick and headed for the street. In her upset the morning before and her desire to get into the office as early as possible, she hadn't run and she'd felt it. Not that the exercise she'd gotten in Patrick's arms hadn't compensated to some extent. But today, given her wakefulness and the fact that she wanted her mind to be clear and alert for the meeting that morning, she set a rapid pace in the cold dawn air of Central Park.

Nearly forty-five minutes and five miles later, she returned to the brownstone half expecting to find Patrick still asleep. It was barely seven. She knew that he'd have to return to his own place before going into the office. What she didn't know was that he'd been awake for half an hour, sitting in the living room, staring at the floor.

Closing the front door very quietly, she turned, then jumped. "Pat! You're up!"

"Mmm." He raised a mug. "Made a pot of coffee. Hoped you wouldn't mind."

He sounded distracted. She assumed he was still half asleep. "Of course not." Crossing the carpet, she leaned forward to kiss his cheek. Her hand slid inside his robe to cover his heart. "You got my note, didn't you?"

"Mmm."

He sounded strange. She couldn't put her finger on it. "Everything okay?"

"Fine."

When she would have questioned him, something held her back. It was bound to be a tense day, what with the board meeting and her continuing campaign against the Widener Corporation. With a frown, she headed for the stairs. "I'll take a quick shower. Be right back."

He was in the same spot when she returned wearing the white robe he'd brought. Her hair was damp, her face still bare of makeup. She stopped before his chair.

"Pat?"

He looked up, jarred from deep thought. "Hmm?"

"Is something wrong?"

"Wrong? Uh, no." But his brow was creased even as he pushed himself from the chair. "I'll give you a hand with breakfast."

She stared after him for a minute before following

him into the kitchen. In silence they made a breakfast of French toast. In silence they ate it. As the clock ticked on, Jordanna knew she should be rushing to get dressed and to the office, but somehow something was happening—or *not* happening—here that was more important. It was only when it occurred to her that Patrick might be having second thoughts about their relationship that she crushed her napkin and looked up.

"What's wrong, Pat? You haven't said two words to me since I got in. *Something's* on your mind. If it's about us—"

Patrick's rising gaze stopped the words at her lips. His intensity pushed them back into her throat and she swallowed hard.

"It is about us. Very much so." At her apprehensive look he raced on. "I want you to marry me."

For more than a minute Jordanna was speechless. Of the things she'd feared he might say, this hadn't been one. "Marry you?" she murmured at last.

His smile had a haunted cast to it. "Is that so hard to believe?"

"Yes. Uh, no. It's...it's just so sudden."

"I know." The urgency was back in his expression. "I hadn't planned it either. I mean, I've known that I loved you for weeks now, but it wasn't until a little while ago that I realized how badly I want to marry you."

"A little while ago?"

"When I woke up it was barely light. It took me a minute to realize where I was. Then I reached for you and you were gone." He took her hand and held it tightly, as though the reminder of that other moment created a new need. "Sheer panic. That was what I felt. Sheer panic. Even after I saw your note, I couldn't stop shaking. I realized then that I have no ties with you. You could very easily get up and walk out of my life.''

"But there *are* ties. I love you!"

"Then marry me! I want to know that you'll always be here, that you'll always be waiting for me."

"Pat," she whispered, slowly shaking her head, "that was what I escaped when I divorced Peter. I won't be the one to sit around and wait—"

His own headshake was vigorous. "Wrong words. Or rather, figuratively offered. It doesn't matter where you are, angel. You can be at the office working your tail off or out at the plant in Tucson. You can be doing whatever you want for as long as is necessary. I wouldn't dream of holding you here. All I need to know is that you'll be thinking of me, that you'll come back to me. I guess after all these years I'm still insecure. I need to know that of all the people you'll run into in a day or a week or a month, I'll come first." He lowered his voice. "Is that selfish?"

"No. Oh, no. It's not selfish. I want it too!"

"Then marry me."

Tears formed in her eyes. Looking down, she clung to his fingers. "It's not selfish to want what you want, to want what *we* want." She raised her eyes. "But it's unfair to ask that of me now. In the past two days, my life has turned upside down. Ten years, Pat. *Ten years*. That's how long I've been living and breathing Willow Enterprises. Suddenly I'm gasping for breath, struggling for survival. I don't know what I would have done if you hadn't come to me yesterday. Even if you hadn't been able to do a thing to help the company, you would have been the comfort I needed. I get strength from you. I never thought I'd say that to a man, never thought I'd allow myself to say it. But it's true. Still, I can't rush into something. We met under unique circumstances at Wild River. You said it yourself. And now, here, the circumstances aren't much less bizarre. I can't think about the future yet. Don't you see? I just can't think straight!"

Wearing a look of defeat, Patrick launched his final plea. "If you love me enough—"

"I *do* love you! But I've been through one marriage and was badly hurt. I want it to be right this time. For *both* our sakes."

Inhaling deeply, he eyed the ceiling, then let out his breath and dropped her hand. "Well, I guess my timing's off." With a look of disgust he stood. "They'd have put me on waivers for this one." Then he started for the stairs.

"Pat?" Jordanna stood.

He didn't turn. "I'd better get dressed. It's late."

She knew how late it was, knew she should be getting dressed as well. Important business faced her at the office. Yet she couldn't follow him upstairs. Instead, she busied herself with cleaning the kitchen. She was standing quietly at the sink, head bowed, when he returned.

"I'm sorry, angel. I shouldn't have upset you. Not today. I know how important this meeting is for you."

He was leaning against the doorjamb. His shirt collar was undone. His tie hung limply in his hand. Looking at him, Jordanna felt her insides melt. Going to him, she wrapped her arms around his waist and pressed her face to his chest.

"Will I...will I see you later?"

"If you want."

She raised her eyes. "Yes. I want."

"Shall I pick you up at the office? Around seven? We could go out for something to eat."

"Seven is fine." She hesitated for just a minute. "Can I call you after the meeting?"

The tense set of his shoulders seemed to relax. "I'd like that. I want to hear how everything went."

She nodded. "Of course. You have an investment—"

"Damn right I do," he cut in, eyes flashing in denial of her preliminary assumption. "I want to make sure you're okay. *You*, Jordanna, first."

Before she could properly comprehend, he kissed her once, briefly but firmly on the mouth, then strode toward the door, scooping up his topcoat in passing, and left.

9

THE MEETING that morning went well. Despite Jordanna's inner turmoil, she looked and acted every bit the self-confident chairman of the board, presenting her case clearly and with conviction. By a unanimous vote, the directors rejected the Widener Corporation's offer, a decision that was promptly put into a letter to be mailed to each of Willow Enterprises' stockholders. Possible defenses against the hostile takeover were discussed, including the search for a friendly buyer. Feeling vaguely uncomfortable, Jordanna related Patrick's offer. The board members were more than open to consider any formal proposal he might submit and agreed to make themselves available for another meeting at short notice.

It was only after the meeting had adjourned, when Jordanna sat back in her office catching her breath, that she pondered her discomfort. Somehow, she felt duplicitous. She felt she hadn't told the board everything. But what should she have said? *The man I love is willing to bail us out? My lover wants to buy in? He's asked me to marry him; wouldn't that be nice—a double merger?*

Life was so complicated. With a touch of self-pity, she wondered why it had to be so.

But there were no answers, not at the moment. There were too many ifs—*if* Patrick could come through with his group, *if* the Widener Corporation gave up the fight, *if* she decided that marriage to Pat was what she truly wanted. She supposed it wouldn't be so bad, when a sufficient amount of time had elapsed, to announce to the board that she and Pat were getting married. Would they wonder, though, if she'd known all along, if she'd set the whole thing up with precisely this in mind? Was there a conflict of interest in her dealing with the Houghton Group?

She needed advice, and Tom Cherwin was the one to call. But such a call was still premature. She needed time. What she'd told Patrick that morning had been the truth. She'd been married once. If she was to marry again, she wanted to know beyond all doubt in the world that it was right and forever.

JORDANNA AND PATRICK had dinner at a quiet French restaurant on the Lower East side, then returned to her place for the night. He didn't mention marriage again, and for that she was grateful. They talked business some; he brought her abreast of his progress on putting together the investors' group and was as optimistic as ever that within several days he'd have a formal proposal to give her board of directors.

Sure enough, after a weekend of quiet intimacy at his townhouse overlooking the East River, Patrick called her on Monday afternoon to present a concrete offer. On one level, Jordanna was ecstatic; his offer was for five dollars a share above what Widener had bid, and the contract provisions were every bit as fair as he'd promised. On another level, though, she knew she had to move.

At her urgent summons, Tom Cherwin arrived in her office within an hour of Patrick's call.

"It sounds good, Jordanna," he admitted after she'd outlined Patrick's proposal. "If we have to merge with someone, we could have done a hell of a lot worse. According to what Clayes has suggested, the Houghton Group will guarantee us nearly complete autonomy." He paused to watch her rise from her desk and approach the window. "Is there a catch?"

"I don't know."

"You don't look as pleased as by rights you should be."

She turned quickly. "Oh, I am pleased. It's just... well... there's something more." She looked at the floor and frowned, searching for the right words, then realized that there weren't any right or wrong words, simply the truth. "Tom, I haven't been as forthright with you as I should have been. I met Patrick Clayes when I was away in New Hampshire last month. We, uh, we've been involved with each other since before this all came up."

"Involved?" Tom echoed, blankly at first. But if the sudden flush on her cheeks hadn't given her away, her evasive gaze would have. "Ahh. Involved." He smiled broadly. "That's wonderful, Jordanna. Is it serious?"

"Very." Bearing infinite worry, her eyes finally met his.

And he understood. "You're concerned about a conflict of interest."

"Yes. He wants me to marry him."

"That's wonderful! Congratulations—"

She held up a hand. "Oh, nothing's happening yet. I haven't said yes. There's too much going on in my life right now to make a decision like that. But it may happen. Someday. And, even if it doesn't, the fact remains that I'm deeply involved with him. At some point, whether Patrick and I ever do marry, the board, the rest of the business world, is apt to find out about us. In the case of the board, they might suspect that I had personal motives for this merger.

As far as the business world goes, can you imagine the hay they'd make of it?''

"I think you're worrying too much about what others will think."

"But that's only part of it. I'm worried about whether I can make an objective judgment where the Houghton Group is concerned.''

"It wouldn't be your decision alone. Anything we decide to do will have to be by majority rule."

"I know. But still.... Tom, I think *you* should be the one to put the proposal before the board. I think *you* should handle this thing from here on."

"You want me to work with the Houghton Group."

"Yes."

"And we tell the board of directors why?"

"It seems the only honest thing to do. And it's an awful lot better than risking their finding out at some later point that Patrick and I are personally involved."

"You know, Jordanna," Tom said, eyeing her over the top of his glasses, "there's nothing wrong with your being personally involved with him. Do you have any idea how many mergers involve family members or friends?''

"I'm sure there are plenty. But at least in those cases the relationship is a known fact."

But Tom was shaking his head. "The only facts that really count in this kind of wheeling and dealing are those written in the contract. Those facts will have to stand by themselves, regardless of your relationship with Clayes."

"That's what I want you to make sure of, Tom. What I'm saying, among other things, is that I'm not sure I wholly trust myself when it comes to Patrick. I may be looking at this deal through rose-colored glasses. What I want is for you to be aware of the situation and to double-check everything. I mean, the Houghton proposal sounds wonderful. It could be precisely what we need. I just want to be sure that's the case." It was like marriage. She wanted it to work.

Tom was nodding. "Of course. I understand."

"I'll explain to the board simply that I'm a close friend of Patrick's and that, for the sake of impartiality, I'll defer to you."

"You're still the president and chairman of the board. They'll want your opinion, Jordanna."

"Oh, they'll have it," she replied with a half smile. "It may be slightly biased—"

"I doubt that," Tom replied, standing to take his leave. "Willow Enterprises means far too much to you to allow for any merger agreement but the best. No, you'd never compromise on the future of the business. I'll get our team to work with Houghton's. We'll have everything in writing before the board meeting."

"I'd like to call it for tomorrow afternoon. Think you can be ready by then?" When Tom raised his brows, she raced on. "With every day that passes Widener is buying more of our stock. According to the reports I'm getting, our major shareholders are standing firm. But there are those minor ones, and they can add up. The sooner we make a counteroffer, the better." She gave a begrudging, "Hmmph. Widener's in luck. If Patrick's offer of fifty-three stands and Shane decides to sell back his shares, Widener will make a bundle. It doesn't seem fair somehow."

"It's the way of Wall Street. We have to accept it."

Watching him leave, Jordanna felt somewhat better. She'd told him about her relationship with Patrick, and he hadn't been shocked or dismayed or incensed. Perhaps she *was* worrying too much.

Patrick said as much that night during dinner. "You didn't have to turn things over to Cherwin. You could've handled it."

"But I feel better this way. At least I'll have ensured myself against any possible future criticism by the board. Don't you see? If I'd said nothing at this stage, I'd be in worse trouble when they found out."

"Are you nervous...about telling them?"

She heard the mild apprehension in Patrick's voice and shared it. "A little. I, uh, I wonder if any of them will comment."

"My guys did."

"They did? You told them about us?"

"My partners. I felt they had a right to know."

"Like my board?"

He nodded. "They thought it was pretty funny that you'd been married to my rival and all."

Jordanna took in his sober expression. "Did it bother you?"

He frowned and took her hand. "A little." He couldn't lie and say he hadn't felt a twinge of anger. "But I got over it. And they had to agree that the deal was sound regardless."

She was silent for a while, studying her hand in his. His fingers were strong, long and firm. No wonder he'd had such control of the football. "I suppose it's something we'll have to learn to live with," she said simply, but she had to wonder if what Patrick had come up against wasn't just the beginning.

ALL THINGS CONSIDERED, the board of directors of Willow Enterprises was remarkably indulgent. At its meeting Tuesday afternoon, Jordanna briefly explained her dilemma before turning the gavel over to Tom. If there were smug remarks to be made, they were kept from her ears. The board voted in overwhelming support of the Houghton proposal, and a messenger was immediately sent to convey the news to the group.

The following morning Patrick filed his statement of intent with the SEC. Ads appeared in the appropriate papers. Jointly signed letters were mailed to the stockholders, accompanied by phone calls to the major ones.

Jordanna was busy. Between those calls conveying her personal endorsement of the agreement with the Houghton Group, and a refocus on the everyday workings of Willow Enterprises, her days were filled to brimming.

As for her nights, they were filled with Patrick. He didn't mention marriage again, but everything he did with, for and to her spoke of his love. Her own blossomed all the more fully, a warm lush feeling that brightened every aspect of her life, binding her to him more and more closely.

They spent every possible minute together, either at home or out. On occasion, in a restaurant, at a party or show, they bumped into people who knew of that earlier link between them. There were comments it was to be expected. For the most part they were positive, offered on a kidding note. Even the small newspaper mention they received simply stated the fact that Jordanna was the former wife of Peter Kirkland, Patrick Clayes's longtime rival. It seemed harmless enough, Jordanna thought. Until she received a call from Peter himself.

"Well," he began in his own inimitably arrogant way, "you're making headlines this time, aren't you, babe?"

She was at the office, deeply involved in a meeting with her marketing vice-president, and was tempted to quickly put him off. But she sensed he had something to say. She knew she had things to say to him. And one phone call from Peter Kirkland was all she wanted to receive.

"Hold on a minute, Peter." She muffled the phone.

"Fifteen minutes, Jill? This has to be taken care of now."

With a smile of understanding, the other woman left. Only when the door was firmly shut behind her did Jordanna remove her hand from the mouthpiece. "How are you, Peter?"

"Surprised, if you want to know the truth. I guess I underestimated you, Jordanna. I didn't think you had it in you."

"What are you talking about?" She had an idea, and didn't like it. But she wanted him to say the words himself.

He proceeded to do just that. "Revenge." It wasn't quite what she'd expected. Eyes wide, she listened as Peter ranted on. "Patrick Clayes. You've really done it, haven't you? Not only are you letting him buy out the company, but you're involved with him personally! I couldn't believe it when Mac called." Mac Heinsohn had been one of Peter's closest playing buddies. Evidently they were still close. "He thought it was pretty funny. I don't."

Jordanna had begun to simmer. "For your information, Patrick is not buying me out. His company is buying *into* Willow Enterprises. There's a difference."

But Peter wasn't listening. "You wanted to get back at me, didn't you? Well, you've done it. How long have you been planning this little coup, Jordanna? Months? Years?"

"If you're as well informed as you claim to be, you'd know that none of this would be happening if Widener hadn't attempted a hostile takeover. That was barely three weeks ago."

"But the two of you—Patrick and you—don't tell me you've only been with him since then."

"We're divorced, Peter. You and I. It seems to me that you shouldn't be concerning yourself with my private life."

"When it affects mine, I'll be as concerned as I want. Hell, Jordanna, I look like a fool."

"Because you couldn't hold me? That's your problem. You were only concerned with yourself. Even now. Nothing's changed."

"What about you, sweetie? Has it ever occurred to you that Clayes gets his revenge too?" Jordanna couldn't believe what he was saying. Her silence tipped Peter off. "God, you're as naive as ever. Well, let me tell you. Clayes wouldn't be doing any of this if it weren't for me."

"That's not true," she argued, but her voice shook as did her limbs.

"Come on," Peter spat. "It's too damn coincidental to be anything else. I have to hand it to the guy. He's pretty clever. Sat around all these years waiting for the right moment. And it fell into his lap. He's a smooth one. You're probably head over heels in love with him. I remember how it was with us. You fell pretty quick then too."

Jordanna called on every bit of the self-control she possessed to keep her voice steady. "I think you've said enough, Peter."

"I don't think so, babe. But then, you never were very good about listening to advice."

"From *whom*? *You*?" She couldn't help herself. Her anger boiled over. "Let me tell *you* something, Peter Kirkland. You know *nothing* when it comes to human beings! You couldn't see an honest emotion if it hit you in the face because you're so damned convinced you have all the answers. Well, you were wrong about me ten years ago. My divorcing you was the smartest thing I ever did. Willow Enterprises gave me back the self-esteem you denied me. If you really want to think that I've built a relationship with Patrick out of revenge, go ahead. You always were self-centered enough to believe that everyone

and everything revolved around you. And that goes
for Patrick's motives too. If you honestly want to believe he's been waiting around all these years simply
for a chance to get back at you, be my guest. But you
know *nothing*, Peter. Patrick is a *man*. Football is
behind him. He's built a very successful life for himself, one that he wouldn't jeopardize for cheap revenge any more than I would."

"So naive," came the caustic retort.

"Not naive," she countered firmly. "Realistic.
And by way of realistic advice, let me suggest that
you simply tell your adoring audience that what
your *ex*-wife does is her business, and her business
alone." She sat straighter. "I haven't got time to hold
your hand if your ego happens to be bruised. I've got
work to do. Now, if you'll excuse me—" Slamming
down the phone, she severed the connection, then
sat trembling in anger for the few minutes it took for
her to regain her composure. When she lifted the
receiver again, it was to buzz Leila.

"Leila, that was my ex-husband. If he calls again,
I'm unavailable. Understood?"

THE DAMAGE HAD BEEN DONE. Jordanna was as furious at
Peter for having suggested what he had as she was
at herself for having listened to him. For, much as
she tried to categorically deny his allegations, she
couldn't totally erase them from her mind.

That night, when she appeared somehow withdrawn, Patrick questioned her.

"What is it, angel? Something's bothering you."

She forced a smile. "Oh, nothing. Just tired, I
guess. Things must be getting to me."

"But everything's going well. Widener's going to
be selling back its stocks. You've nothing to fear
from them anymore."

But from you? she wanted to ask, but didn't. She

knew she should come right out and tell him about Peter's call. Somehow she couldn't. She was embarrassed. Patrick would think she didn't trust him at all. She was frightened. What if some of what Peter had said was true?

They didn't make love that night. Patrick simply held her in his arms until, at last, she fell asleep. Long after, he lay worrying, fearing that it was the intensity of their relationship that was getting to her. He thought about cooling it for a while, but he couldn't. He needed to see her, to speak with her, to be with her. As it was, he was exercising the greatest control in not pestering her about marriage. More than anything in the world, he wanted her to be his wife. With each day, the need grew. And it was never more dire than at times like this when he realized just how unattached she truly was.

THEN CAME THE DAY, nearly a month after the agreement with the Houghton Group had been formalized, when Jordanna had to go to St. Louis. She'd put the trip off twice, just as Patrick had limited himself to day trips so that they might have the nights to themselves and each other. But she couldn't delay it longer. Her plant manager was resigning and his replacement had to be interviewed and approved. When hiring was done at such an important level, Jordanna had always reserved the final judgment for herself after her personnel department had narrowed the field to the three top contenders. This time, given the fact that she'd have to be away from Patrick for two nights, her heart wasn't in it. But her mind was. Particularly in light of the recent changes in the ownership of Willow Enterprises, she knew that this was no time to abdicate her responsibility. As a show of command, if nothing more, she had to go.

The parting was difficult for Jordanna, enlightening in its way. Patrick accompanied her to the airport for the early-morning flight.

"Are you sure you'll be okay?" he asked, hands firmly gripping the lapels of her coat as they stood by the boarding gate.

"I'll be fine. I've done this many times before."

"I know, but still...." He cast a worried glance through the sheets of glass. "It looks like it might snow. They're predicting it."

She laughed softly. "By the time it comes, I'll be up there above it all. You're the one who'll be stuck with it."

"I wish you'd let me come."

They'd discussed this before. "You've got your own work to do, Pat. And I've got to let our people down there know that I'm still firmly in control. No, it's better that I go alone." Her voice cracked. "Though I will miss you."

Enfolding her in his arms, Patrick held her tightly. "I'll miss you too, angel. You'll call when you're free?"

"Every night."

Boarding began. While the other passengers flowed by, he held her silently. When they could put it off no longer, he kissed her. "I love you, Jordanna."

She buried her face against his neck, breathing deeply of him for a final time. "I love you too."

"Will you...?" His voice trailed off with indecision.

"Will I what?"

Unable to stop himself, he went ahead. "Will you think about us while you're there?" The slight emphasis he put on the *us* left no doubt in Jordanna's mind what he referred to.

"I will," she whispered.

"And you'll behave?"

"I will." Reaching up, she kissed him once more.

Then, fearful she might lose her composure altogether, she quickly hoisted her shoulder bag and
headed for the door.

Patrick watched, feeling helpless and empty as she
walked away from him. Her departure was a harsh
reminder of precisely how much she meant to him.
She was his light. Without her his world was dark
and lonely.

As PROMISED, Jordanna called him that night. She told
him about the flight, which had been smooth, and
about the interviews she'd had with two of the three
finalists that afternoon at the plant. These had been
more perplexing. Something was missing in each of
the two men she'd interviewed. She couldn't put her
finger on it. Intuition, she told Pat. He simply
chuckled when she tried to apologize and told her
that her intuition was very definitely something to
be trusted. Hadn't it gotten her this far in life, he
asked. She wondered.

The third interview was scheduled for the following morning, after which she had meetings scheduled with various of the plant personnel and the
decision on the manager to make. On the third
morning, she would have a meeting with the chosen
one. In her briefcase she carried detailed reports on
each of the candidates; these she reviewed time and
again.

From the moment she sat down with the third
candidate, she knew what her decision would be.
She also knew what had been missing in the other
two men. A plant manager, *her* plant manager, had
to be ultrasensitive to people. This third man had
called half an hour before he was due to come, saying that there was an emergency at the plant he was
presently managing and that he might be several
minutes late. He wasn't. But he explained his call.

One of his workers had collapsed on the job. He'd wanted to be sure that the woman was taken to the right hospital, that she was given immediate attention by the best doctor and that her family was gently notified and on their way.

Jordanna hired him on the spot. Intuition, she told herself, not to mention the fact that his qualifications had been impeccable, his references superb. Or was it simply that, with the decision made and the congratulatory meeting held there and then, she was free to fly back to New York that night?

She didn't stop to analyze her motives, but pushed herself headlong into the afternoon's meetings. She was tired but enthusiastic when she called Pat to tell him of her change in plans. He was delighted. There was no way he could have fabricated his pleasure, she told herself, even if he *had* had reason to do so. If, as Peter had so callously suggested, he had sought her and her business out of revenge, by rights Patrick would have been looking forward to this break from her. But she believed him when he said he loved her, when he said he missed her, when he said he'd be there at the airport to meet her at whatever time the plane touched down.

In a state of immense satisfaction, she took a cab to the airport. Several of the plant personnel had offered to drive her, but she'd wanted the time alone. Nothing, no one, should intrude on her thoughts of Patrick, she decided. She was going home.

The plane was filled. She'd been fortunate to get a last-minute seat. Buckling herself in, she put her head back and took a deep breath, then awaited the takeoff. It went without a hitch, right on time, smooth and, for Jordanna, with promise.

St. Louis was no more than an hour behind when that promise was shattered by the quiet announcement from the captain.

"Ladies and gentlemen." He cleared his throat. "I'm afraid we'll be taking a slight detour. There's a gentleman here in the cockpit with us who insists on being taken elsewhere. He may be armed." There was a break before his voice returned more tensely. "He is armed but wants no harm to come to any of us. On his behalf, I ask you to remain calm. I'll keep you informed of our flight plan once it is determined."

Jordanna sat in her seat as a wave of disbelief, then fear, swept the large cabin. *Hijack*. The word was a murmur, bouncing in a wave from one row of seats to another. Flight attendants moved deftly up and down the aisles, their pale faces in contrast to the smooth words of assurance they delivered on cue.

Hijack. It seemed unreal. But then, so had *takeover* been, and she'd seen the end results of that. A slow trembling started deep within Jordanna, seeping steadily through her limbs until she had to grasp the upholstered arms on either side for support.

Hijack? Was it possible? After everything she'd been through during the past few months, it couldn't be! She looked frantically from side to side but found nothing reassuring in the faces around her. Those too were pale and searching hers for the answers none of them had.

"This is too much," the man on her left muttered. "I've been flying for thirty years and nothing like this has ever happened. I mean, I've had engines go dead. I've had lightning all but strike the plane. But...a hijacking?"

"The worst that's ever happened to me," ventured the younger man on Jordanna's right, "was to lose my luggage. It went to Greece while I went to California. I had to go out and buy new clothes. My bags made it two days later."

Eyes straight ahead and dazed, Jordanna heard herself join the conversation. "I was supposed to fly home tomorrow. This was a last-minute change of plans. I wanted to be back. I thought—" She stopped talking when a lump formed in her throat. Sensing the state of her emotions, the man on her left patted her hand in a fatherly fashion. In other circumstances, she might have thought it condescending— the little lady needing comfort. But she did need comfort. And she appreciated the gesture.

"How can this kind of thing happen?" the man on her right demanded of no one in particular. "My God, with all the security precautions at airports you'd think they'd be able to prevent it. Everything goes through X-rays. How could some kook walk up there and say he's armed?"

"Maybe he's bluffing," the man on her left conjectured. "They're probably trying to find that out now."

"Either that, or they're trying to talk him out of it," Jordanna offered, trying to gather her wits and assess the situation in whatever small manner she could. It was hard. Her stomach was in knots and her thoughts kept wandering, mostly toward New York where Patrick would soon be waiting. Incredulous still, she shook her head. "Where do you think he wants to go?"

"Cuba?" suggested the man on her right. In vague macho fashion, he was wearing jeans and a Western-style shirt. Jordanna thought him to be in his mid-twenties and prayed that he—or any other of the passengers—wouldn't be so foolish as to try to storm the cockpit.

"Maybe the Middle East," suggested the man on her left. "If we land in a country we have no extradition treaty with, a hijacker would be safe."

Jordanna looked over at him. Perhaps in his early

fifties, he wore a business suit and might have seemed perfectly calm except for the sweat that dotted his forehead. When he met her gaze, she gave him a worried smile and looked down. Again he patted her hand. Again she welcomed the kind gesture.

Very slowly, the shock aboard the craft gave way to a thick, quiet tension. What conversation there was was muted. All ears were attuned to the moment the captain's voice would return. The flight attendants came through bearing drinks, explaining that dinner would be served later. It went without saying that the food provisions might have to be stretched somewhat, depending on their final destination.

It seemed an eternity before the captain came back on the loudspeaker. His voice was low, obviously strained. A ripple of apprehension passed through the cabin. All other noise ceased.

"This is your captain speaking. I've just been given clearance to head for Philadelphia, where we'll be stopping briefly to refuel. If there are any medical conditions that need special attention, please notify one of the flight attendants now. Once we leave Philadelphia, we'll be heading for Benghazi."

With a curt click, the speaker went dead. In its wake, silence reigned, but only long enough for the passengers to absorb this new bit of information.

"Benghazi?" the man on Jordanna's right echoed. "Where in the hell is *that*?"

"Libya," returned the man on her left in a dull tone of voice. "It's on the other side of the world!"

"Should've been Cuba," the first growled. "Would've been faster, cleaner."

Wearily, Jordanna closed her eyes and withered into her seat. Libya. It *was* on the other side of the world. So far away from Patrick. So far away from everything she knew that was safe and predictable. God only knew what the Libyans would do with an American aircraft jammed with people! God only knew if they'd make it there in one piece!

Suddenly the world seemed a very bleak place with the only bright light shining from New York. Patrick would be there, waiting, worrying. But she'd be landing in Philadelphia, so close, so very close, then taking off again for Africa and a far and hostile land. What was in store for her—for the entire planeload of people—was unknown and therefore terrifying. Most terrifying of all was the thought that, should something go wrong, she might never see Patrick again.

10

PATRICK STOOD AT THE ARRIVAL GATE in a state of disbelief. "What did you say?"

"We don't know when that flight will be in," the young airline official repeated softly, apologetically. "It's been hijacked."

"Hijacked. You've got to be kidding."

"I wish I were."

Patrick made a face. *"Hijacked?"*

"The plane should be landing in Philadelphia right about now. It'll refuel there."

"And then?"

The woman's voice lowered. "They'll go on to Libya."

"Libya! This has to be a joke."

The woman shook her head.

"You're serious?" When she nodded, his heart skipped a beat. "Oh, my God!"

"I'm sorry, sir. We're doing everything we can to try to talk the man out of it."

Patrick's eyes flashed. "How could something like this happen? I thought you people were so careful!"

"We are," she replied as calmly as she could. "The captain says the man's got an explosive hooked to his pacemaker."

"Pacemaker!" Patrick cried, then dropped his voice an octave. "This is too much."

"We had no way of knowing. Since the man couldn't pass through the metal detectors, he was searched by hand. The pacemaker was an external one, secured near his waist. No one ever dreamed it wasn't legitimate.''

"No one ever dreamed...." Patrick muttered. "Damn it, my woman's on that plane!"

The official tossed a pained glance toward the other people somberly clustered at the arrival gate. "They've got friends and relatives on it too. I'm sorry. I wish there were more I could say. There's no reason to believe that the plane won't land in Benghazi, drop the hijacker and then quickly return here. If you'd like to wait, we'll fill you in on any news as we get it.''

"Wait. Uh, yes, I'll wait." His brow furrowed, then cleared as he tried to sort out his whirling thoughts. "How long? How long will it take to get to Benghazi and back?''

When she grew flustered, a male official stepped in. "The flying time one way is close to thirteen hours.''

"Thirteen hours! And they'll have enough fuel?'' He could just see the plane running out midway, and shuddered.

"It'll be close, but they should be okay. If necessary they can land in Tripoli, but the hijacker insists on going to Benghazi. If the Libyans allow them to land and take right off again—"

"*If,*" Patrick interrupted in anger. "But if the Libyan government detains them...."

The official shook his head once. "We have no reason to believe that the Libyans would detain them for any reason. Please, sir. There's no cause for immediate alarm.''

"*No cause?* My God, man! This isn't exactly your average flight!'' He looked down, eyes terror filled. "Hijacked. It can't be. Jordanna's on that plane.'' Suddenly he looked back up. "Maybe she's not. She only got a seat at the last minute. Maybe it was overbooked...or she missed it...."

"Her name?" Already the official was studying the clipboard before him.

"Kirkland," Patrick stated, heart pounding. "Jordanna Kirkland."

One page of names was studied, then turned. Patrick's hopes rose. He didn't care if she hadn't called. Or maybe she had; he'd been out of the office since he received her first call and had wanted to get to the airport in plenty of time. He didn't care if she'd have to take tomorrow's flight after all. Just as long as she was safe.

But his hopes were shattered when the official pressed a finger midway down the second sheet of paper. "Jordanna Kirkland. Yes, I'm afraid she is on the flight."

Patrick squeezed his eyes shut. The young woman came from behind the counter to gently take his elbow. "Why don't you have a seat, sir? We'll have coffee brought out in a little while. As soon as we hear anything, we'll pass it on."

Dumbly he looked at her, then followed her glance toward the others waiting in small, quiet groups. "Uh, yes. I think...I think I'll just go stand by the window."

"If there's anything we can get you...."

"Get me Jordanna," he ordered. "Just get her back here safely."

"We'll do our best," the woman offered softly, then left him to give her attention to another worried party that approached.

Patrick stared out the window for what seemed an eternity. Disbelief, shock, anger—each yielded in turn to the next. When at last he turned and took a seat, he was filled with an awful helplessness. And fear. So much could happen. A hijacker had to be crazy to begin with. What if he completely lost his mind midflight and detonated the explosive he carried? What if someone tried to tackle him and the explosive went off by accident? What if the Libyans detained both the plane and its crew. Torture? Mayhem? Or if they refused to grant the hijacker asylum and he went berserk there and then?

Beads of sweat covered Patrick's brow. He mopped them with his forearm, then thrust his fingers through his hair. It was unreal! All of it! Jordanna was coming back to him, *rushing* back to him. She'd advanced her schedule, taken an earlier flight. For him. Guilt joined terror to consume him. If anything happened to her, he'd never forgive himself. Why couldn't it have been *he* on that plane? Why Jordanna? Why now, just when things were looking so good for them?

Hours passed. The terminal slowly filled with anxious friends and relatives, silent in their vigil. Representatives of the media quietly worked the crowd, interviewing those who would speak, deftly bypassing others. Standing once more at the window with his back to the rest, Patrick waited angrily, almost daring someone from the press to approach him. He'd tell them what he thought, crude bastards. To shove a microphone at a person who was obviously in pain was low and dirty and heartless.

"Got someone on it too?"

Snapping his head to the side, Patrick found himself glaring at an elderly gentleman whose eyes were moist. Instantly contrite, he curbed his anger and nodded

The man gripped the wood rail with gnarled hands that shook slightly. "My daughter's on it. Didn't even know it until my son-in-law had the good grace to call. We're not close." There was sadness in his broken voice and regret. "Heard about it on the eleven o'clock news. Never imagined she'd be aboard."

"Did the news have anything to add that we don't know?" Patrick asked as gently as he could, but there was an underlying urgency in his tone that he couldn't hide. Despite hourly updates by airport personnel, real news had been scarce. The plane was indeed en route to Libya. Beyond that, nothing was known.

The old man shook his head. "Just mention of some of the passengers. A singer. Never heard of him. Couple of company presidents. Never heard of them either. Course, no one's heard of my Jane."

Patrick wondered if Jordanna's name had been mentioned, but he didn't ask. It didn't matter. The only thing that mattered was that the plane and its passengers should return intact. And soon.

In as blind a daze as Patrick felt himself, the old man wandered off. A long table had been set up at one end of the room with sandwiches and hot drinks. The thought of food made Patrick sick. He wondered if Jordanna had eaten, wondered whether there'd be enough food and drink to sustain the passengers through their ordeal. He tried to remember what he'd read about other hijackings, but drew a blank. Slamming his fist upon the rail, he gritted his teeth against the pain. But the worst of the pain was inside, and it only grew as the long night wore on.

By dawn, he felt desolate. Slumped in a chair, he watched the sky pale. Around him, others shifted and fidgeted. Those who'd fallen asleep awoke with urgently whispered inquiries about news. Those who'd gone home for the night slowly trickled back.

Helping himself to a cup of hot coffee, Patrick wandered aimlessly about the room. He felt, in turn, like a caged animal, then a grateful hostage. Rubbing a hand to his shadowed jaw, he wondered if he should go home to shave and shower. But he didn't want to go anywhere. Not while Jordanna was out there. Not while there might be news.

At nine in the morning, slouched once more in a seat, he was roused from his depression by a familiar voice.

"Pat! I just heard!" Andrew Harper, one of his partners and close friends, slipped breathlessly into the seat next to him. "I got here as soon as I could."

"You heard?" Patrick echoed, numb.

"Read, actually. The newspaper." He held a copy folded in his lap, but Patrick was too weary to reach for it.

"They mentioned her?"

"Yes. She's one of several big names on the plane."

Patrick thought of the old man who'd talked with him hours before. "They're all big names, Andy. Every one of them—" he tossed his head toward the crowd behind him "—to these people here."

Andrew looked appropriately chastised. Then he eyed his friend cautiously. "Is there any news? The paper simply said the plane was on its way to Libya."

"It should be arriving within the hour." Word had come through a few minutes before. "That's all we know."

"Well, at least that's something. They're getting there."

Patrick shuddered and stared straight ahead. "Now we have to wonder what the Libyans will do with them. Once they land, they'll probably sit on a runway sweltering in the heat. If the hijacker remains on board, they'll be in continuing danger from him. If he gets off, they may be in danger from the Libyans." Leaning forward, he knotted his hands together. "All we can do is to pray that the plane will be allowed to take off with everyone but the hijacker aboard."

Andrew raised a hand to his friend's shoulder. "It'll get off okay. You'll see."

Patrick closed his eyes tightly. "I keep thinking of Entebbe. What those people went through—"

"That was a political thing, Pat. This is not. It's one crazy man. The Libyans wouldn't do anything to risk this country's retaliation."

Opening his eyes wide, Patrick sat back with a tired sigh. "I keep telling myself that but, damn it, it doesn't help. Jordanna's on that plane. If it weren't for me, she'd have flown in safely this morning. If anything happens to her, I don't think I'll ever forgive myself. Not to mention the idea of living without her—"

"Hell, Pat. Since when were you such a pessimist?"

Patrick looked at his friend then. "I'm talking reality."

"You're talking morbid. Hey, when was the last time you heard of an American plane being hijacked with anything happening to either its passengers or crew?" When Patrick thought for a minute, then shrugged, Andrew went on. "They'll all be okay. Sure, maybe hot. Maybe tired and hungry and thirsty. But they'll be okay. Got that?"

"I have your word?" Patrick asked, sarcasm in his arched brow.

Andrew simply sent him a chiding glance, then softened. "Is there anything I can do?" Pat shook his head. "I'll cover you at the office. Any important meetings that can't be postponed?"

Nothing was so important that it couldn't be postponed. Not when Jordanna was in danger. Again he shook his head.

"You really should go home and change. You look awful."

Pat was still shaking his head. "I can't. Not yet, at

least. Once we get word that the plane's on the way home, I may leave for an hour." He glanced at his watch. He'd calculated and recalculated all night. "In the most optimistic circumstances, they could be back tonight. Until I know something, anything, I'm staying here."

"Want me to stop back later?"

Pat's smile was sad but it held his appreciation. "No. Thanks anyway, Andy. I'll just...sit here. I'll be okay. Don't worry about me."

"You're sure?"

"Yup."

But he began to wonder as the day dragged on. There was no news, other than that the plane had indeed landed in Benghazi. No word of a takeoff. No word of a seizure. Nothing. Patrick's frustration was shared by the others standing watch. His worry was reflected on their faces, his sense of helplessness in the way they seemed to wander in aimless circles, sitting, only to stand and walk again.

When, at midafternoon, a reporter approached him, he was too tired to muster immediate fight.

"Excuse me," the young woman said, "but aren't you...you look very much like...."

"I am," he conceded, staring off toward the runways he'd already imprinted inch by inch on his mind.

"Do you have someone on this flight, Mr. Clayes?"

"Yes. My woman."

The reporter began to write.

"Must you do that?" Patrick snapped, tossing a glance over his shoulder. "Have you made notes on each of these people and the names of those they're waiting for?"

"Some," the reporter returned calmly.

"And you've asked how they feel, whether they're worried?"

"Logical questions, given the circumstances."

"Doesn't it occur to you that this is an invasion of privacy? That they may not want someone poking her nose in at such an awful time?"

"It's news, Mr. Clayes. You should know that."

"Oh, I know it, all right, which is why I always did avoid the press." Standing, he thrust his fists into his pants pockets. "If you'll excuse me...." Without another word, he walked off.

It was shortly after five when a somber-faced airline representative announced that the plane had not yet left Libya. Renewed expressions of anxiety rippled through the air. Patrick stood stiffly while the representative explained that both the airline and the government were doing everything they could. Turning, head bowed, Patrick walked to the window once more.

How was Jordanna? She had to be exhausted. And frightened. If he thought the waiting hard, he could barely begin to imagine what *she* had to be going through. Nearly twenty-four hours—that was how long she'd been on the plane. *If* she was still on the plane. He shuddered when he thought of the alternatives, then tried to think more positively. Most likely there was some simply explained delay. But what? Red tape? *Why hadn't the plane taken off?*

Dropping into a chair, Patrick realized that he was more bone tired than he'd ever been in his life. He felt as though he'd played three football games back-to-back and then had been forced to run around the entire field a dozen times. Moreover, those games had been Super Bowls and he'd blown each one.

Nothing, no, *nothing* could compare with the way he felt. Worried. Fearful. Empty. Alone. The others waiting so tensely in the terminal might have been some comfort; sharing the ordeal, there was a gentle bond between them. But he couldn't share his thoughts with them, didn't want to hear their tales of woe. Rather, he drew into himself and centered his thoughts on willing Jordanna safe and well.

Six o'clock became seven. The winter's night had long since fallen. Seven became eight, then nine. The crowd thinned out again as some of its members went home for a few hours' rest. Patrick dozed once or twice in his seat, only to snap awake to a vision of an explosion or gunfire and screams. Andrew stopped by again and tried to persuade him to go home for a bit, but Patrick was adamant about not leaving until he heard something positive.

Finally, at three in the morning word came. With a ration of fuel, the plane had taken off from Benghazi and, after a stop in Gibraltar for food, drink and sufficient extra fuel to see it across the Atlantic, would be heading home. The words were sweet, bringing tears of anguished relief to all eyes in the room, including Patrick's. Numb with fatigue, but elated by the promise of having Jordanna in his arms that night, he finally left the airport and went home.

By the time he returned, with several hours' sleep, a shave, shower and fresh clothes to his credit, he felt almost human. Almost. The rest would come when Jordanna was back with him.

The atmosphere at the arrival gate was one of quiet excitement. With word from Gibraltar not only that the plane had left there on schedule but also that everyone aboard was well, if tired, the friends and relatives who waited in New York broke out in smiles from time to time. But an air of guardedness remained; not until the plane actually touched down would anyone fully rejoice.

As afternoon became evening, the crowd swelled. Joining those who had so faithfully kept the long vigil were other family members and friends. Moving from group to group in scavenger fashion were representatives from both the print and electronic media.

Patrick kept to himself for the most part, eyes glued to the sky. As the minutes passed, his excitement grew. The plane was due in at six. With a mere fifteen minutes to go, and the sun a faint memory in the west, he turned from the window to get a drink of water, only to stop, dead still and stare ahead. There, looking fresh and alert, chatting amiably with two reporters, was Peter Kirkland.

Patrick's first response was to haul back and punch the man in the mouth. He'd come for the show, the bastard! He intended to cash in on Jordanna's ordeal, to milk it for whatever publicity he could get!

Then Peter met his gaze with a message that was hard and direct. Patrick looked away, then back, then away again, deep in thought. When he looked back a final time, it was to calmly nod to Peter. Very deliberately he unclenched his hand and tucked it comfortably into the pocket of his slacks. Then, accepting the challenge Peter had issued, he went for his drink of water.

As the landing time grew closer, a sense of anticipation filled the arrival area. Ignoring Peter Kirkland's presence and the press contingent he courted, Patrick stood at a far side of the room, alternately watching the lighted runway and the information monitor suspended from the ceiling. The minutes seemed endless. Somehow fatigue was forgotten, as was the anguish that had dominated the past two days. In their place was an excitement just waiting to bubble and overflow.

When the airline official announced that the plane had touched down and would be approaching the terminal momentarily, a collective sigh of relief seemed to waft into the air, accompanied by random cheers and an exultant shout. The crowd inched forward, restrained in its joy only by airline personnel who struggled to leave an open path for the passengers.

Patrick remained at the side. Given his superior height, he could easily see the door through which the passengers would pass. Likewise, he knew Jordanna would easily see him.

Heart thudding, he caught sight of the aircraft's lights as it pulled up to the terminal. His throat felt suddenly tight; he tried to swallow the lump there but couldn't. All he could do was to imagine the airplane's door being opened and its passengers, who'd traveled such a long way, streaming out, up the corridor, onto home soil at last.

It seemed an eternity before the first of the bedraggled travelers emerged to be crushed into familiar, welcoming arms. Patrick's eyes filled with tears; he brushed them with his sleeve and focused again, waiting, watching, his life suspended until she came into view.

Inside the aircraft, Jordanna waited for those before her to begin to move. She wondered how something so simple could take so long, particularly after all they'd been through, then realized that, exhausted as she was, her patience was next to nil. Those around her were as quiet as she; it was as though every bit of the energy they possessed was focused on terra firma and home. She shifted from her left foot to her right, then hoisted the strap of her shoulder bag more comfortably when, at last, the line started forward.

She needed to see Patrick, needed to hold him. Had it not been for thought of him, she might have gone mad during the harrowing hours of flight, the more harrowing hours of silent detainment on Libyan soil. If she'd needed something to help her sort things out regarding her life, this ordeal had been it. Forty-eight hours of enforced inactivity, of near constant fear, could do that to a person. Oh, yes, she knew what she wanted. It was simply a matter of physically getting there.

She thought she'd scream when the line slowed down again, but it moved on again quickly and, heart pounding, she kept up. Weary as she was, both mentally and physically, she suddenly had all the energy in the world. It was as though her life passed through a funnel, narrowing in on the one element that held meaning. Patrick.

The corridor leading from the plane into the terminal seemed endless. The clamor of joyous reunions reached her moments before she stepped into the light. Blood thundering through her veins, she searched the throng of faces. Tears blurred her vision. Walking ever forward, she blinked.

"Jordanna! Over here!" She turned her head to see a large man approaching. But it wasn't Patrick. It was... *Peter.* The nightmare continued!

Before she could move much farther, she was enveloped in a hug expansive enough to be captured by the cameras that rolled. "How are you, babe? I was so worried!"

Frantic now, she continued to search the crowd. Peter kissed her soundly on her cheek, but she didn't notice. Could it be that Patrick hadn't come? Could it be that her ordeal had been for nothing? Tears streaming down her cheeks, she struggled to focus.

Then she saw him, as different from Peter as night from day. Where Peter looked fresh and well rested, Patrick was the one who had obviously lived through the ordeal with her. Where Peter was surrounded by the press, Patrick stood alone, waiting in anguish.

"I've got to go," she heard herself murmur, and

pushed against Peter's arms. "Excuse me...I've got to...." Then she was free, dodging her way through the crowds, until at last Patrick was holding her and she knew she was home.

Heavy sobs came from deep within then, expressing both the heartache she'd endured and the joy of reunion. Her arms circled his neck, clinging with desperation and need and love. She couldn't talk through her tears, could only hold him tighter, and tighter. He was as silent, and as firm. His strong arms surrounded her. His own tears fell freely.

How long they stood like that, they neither knew nor cared. The only thing that mattered was that they were together again. Gathering his composure mere moments ahead of her, Patrick moved his lips by her ear. His voice was hoarse, but she heard every word. "There's a diamond ring in my pocket. Want it?"

Face buried still against his neck, right arm remaining coiled in tight possession, she lowered her left hand to his pocket. The small box was easily opened, her finger quickly slid through the ring. Then, without so much as a look at the exquisite gem, she resumed her hold of him.

"I love you, Pat. I love you so much!"

"Mrs. Kirkland. A moment, please?" The interruption came from one of the several press people who'd gathered around. Jordanna pressed her head more tightly to Patrick's neck. "How was it?" came the intrusive voice. "Did the passengers ever panic?"

"Did the Libyans board the plane?" demanded a second.

"Did you talk with the hijacker at all?" shot a third.

Very slowly and with deliberation, Patrick eased Jordanna to his side. Wiping the tears from her cheeks, he broke out into a broad smile. "I love you," he mouthed, rewarded by her own smile. Then he turned to the microphones that seemed to have gathered in a swarm. "I believe that Mrs. Kirkland is well, but tired. She's been through an ordeal. We've *all* been through an ordeal."

"She saw her husband—" a reporter began, only to be soundly interrupted by Patrick, whose gaze had returned to Jordanna's and was not to be dislodged.

"Her *ex*-husband. She's engaged to me now."

"Engaged?" A second reporter frowned down at his notebook as though in search of information he'd somehow missed.

"That's right," Patrick said with a grin.

Sniffing a new story in the works, an astute television correspondent waved his microphone closer. "So the rivalry goes on?"

Patrick's grin didn't fade, nor did he shift his eyes from Jordanna's. "No. The rivalry's over. Now, if you'll excuse us...." Turning, he began to lead Jordanna from the crowd.

A final question followed them. "When's the wedding?"

"Within the month," Patrick stated, his arm wrapped firmly about Jordanna's shoulders as he quickened his pace. "Is that all right?" he murmured softly, when at last the reporters had given up.

"Oh, yes," she breathed, her bright eyes beaming. "Oh...yes."

"Hɪ, sleepyhead," Patrick whispered, smiling broadly. "How do you feel?"

Opening her other eye, Jordanna stretched, then reached forward and took his hands. "Better. I was exhausted."

"Good reason for that." His eyes lowered briefly

before returning to her face. "Maybe you should cut back your hours."

She smiled at his concern. "I already have. And I'm okay. Really. A nap before dinner always does the trick. Have you been sitting here long?"

"Long enough. I like watching you. My beautiful wife." Leaning forward, he caught her lips in an exquisitely gentle kiss.

"Mmm," Jordanna breathed. "I like that." In the eighteen months they'd been married, it had only gotten better and better.

"Angel?"

She opened her eyes to find him looking at her in concern.

"Are you sure this is what you want?"

Laughing, she pressed his hand to her swelling stomach. "It's a little late to worry about that, isn't it?" She was six months pregnant and growing by the day.

"But I do worry. I know how much the business means—"

Leaving his hand on their child, she put her fingers to his lips. "Shh. I thought I'd made that clear. The business is . . . the business. You're my life. And now we'll have a child to love." She paused. "You're not sorry, are you?" She recalled her first marriage and the reluctance Peter had had to share any part of her. In her heart she knew Patrick was different. Still, from time to time, she needed to hear the words. As had always been the case in the past, she wasn't disappointed now.

"God, no! I've dreamed about having this baby. You know that." Raising the edge of her loose blouse, he leaned low to kiss her rounded belly. "I love you so much I think I'll burst at times. It'll be a relief to have someone to absorb the overflow."

For Jordanna, it was the same. Threading her

fingers into his hair, she held his head as he brushed his lips back and forth over her flesh. When he gently gripped the elastic band of her pants and eased it down, she closed her eyes against the heady pleasure.

"Oh, Pat, I love you," she whispered, then caught her breath when his lips moved lower. And lower. Suddenly her pulse was racing at the excitement of his touch. "Pat, let's—"

"Shh. Let me."

And he did. Using his lips and tongue and those phenomenally agile fingers of his, he brought her to the furthest reaches of desire and back, before at last sliding up her trembling body.

"You're wonderful," he murmured, careful not to hurt her as he moved his large body over hers.

It took her a moment to catch her breath. But it was hard, given the sensual rock of his body. "Patrick," she chided, "you're fully dressed."

"Not for long." Grinning, he reached for the buckle of his belt. "Not for long."

When he took her then, it was with precious care and tenderness. She enveloped him, gave him every bit as much of herself back, and then some. He was first in her life. It had been that way since the moment they'd set eyes on each other in the woods of New Hampshire. If it was reassurance he sought, Jordanna intended to spend a lifetime and beyond giving him precisely that. For in the giving she received. It was what their love was all about.

Harlequin Announces...

Harlequin Superromance™
NEW

IMPROVED EXCELLENCE

Beginning with February releases (titles #150 to #153) each of the four Harlequin Superromances will be 308 pages long and have a regular retail price of $2.75 ($2.95 in Canada).

The new shortened Harlequin Superromance guarantees a faster-paced story filled with the same emotional intensity, character depth and plot complexity you have come to expect from Harlequin Superromance.

The tighter format will heighten drama and excitement, and that, combined with a strong well-written romance, will allow you to become more involved with the story from start to finish.

WATCH FOR A SPECIAL INTRODUCTORY PRICE ON HARLEQUIN SUPERROMANCE TITLES #150–#153 IN FEBRUARY

Available wherever paperback books are sold or through Harlequin Reader Service:

In the U.S.
P.O. Box 52040
Phoenix, AZ 85072-2040

In Canada
P.O. Box 2800, Postal Station A
5170 Yonge Street
Willowdale, Ontario M2N 6J3